"If the cap fits—"

April couldn't keep the irony from her voice.

A flash of fury swept across Hugh's features. "Would you prefer I give in to every whim I get, every urge I feel?"

April was shocked by his unexpected anger.

"Tomorrow we head back to Sydney," he went on quite savagely, "and in two days' time I'll be in that hospital, having that operation. I hate the uncertainty, the doubts—hate the way it all makes me feel weak, helpless!"

"Oh, Hugh, you shouldn't—"

"Shouldn't what?" he snapped. "April, I'm going mad with worry, not to mention—" He broke off, running a shaking hand through his hair. "I crave a distraction. What do you suggest I do—race you off for a quickie? If you're as sexy as your perfume, I'd surely sleep afterward."

MIRANDA LEE was born and brought up in New South Wales, Australia. She had a brief career as cellist in an orchestra, and then another as a computer programmer. A move to the country after marriage and the birth of the first of three daughters limited her career opportunities to being a full-time wife and mother. Encouraged by her family, she began writing in 1982. She favors a well-paced what-happens-next kind of story, but says what matters most "is that my books please and entertain my readers, leaving them feeling good and optimistic about love and marriage in our present topsy-turvy world."

Books by Miranda Lee

HARLEQUIN PRESENTS

MIRANDA LEE

the reluctant lover

Harlequin Books

TORONTO • NEW YORK • LONDON
AMSTERDAM • PARIS • SYDNEY • HAMBURG
STOCKHOLM • ATHENS • TOKYO • MILAN
MADRID • WARSAW • BUDAPEST • AUCKLAND

Harlequin Presents first edition August 1992
ISBN 0-373-11481-8

Original hardcover edition published in 1991
by Mills & Boon Limited

THE RELUCTANT LOVER

CHAPTER ONE

APRIL slid open the glass doors and stepped out on to the wooden decking. She moved over to the railing and leant against it, letting her tired eyes feast on the serene beauty before her. The clean white sand, the clear blue-green water... The Pacific Ocean at its best!

Uncle Guy had been so right. A couple of weeks up here at his beach-house, all alone, was exactly what she needed before getting back to the grind-stone of her last year at university.

She glanced idly down to the other end of the secluded cove, to the only other house for miles, calm in the knowledge that its owner would not be in occupancy.

'Oh, no,' she groaned. A light was coming from one of the windows of the cliff-hugging dwelling. And yes... there was a man standing at the water's edge.

Her stomach twisted. Uncle Guy had said that Max had gone overseas. She wouldn't have come otherwise.

April strained her eyes in a vain attempt to recognise the man, but he was too far away.

The distant figure turned and began strolling towards her end of the beach. April shaded her eyes from the rays of the setting sun and peered hard.

His hair colour was similar to Max's. Fairish. And he looked just as tall.

Her agitation grew. If it *was* Max she would turn right round and drive back to Sydney.

The man drew nearer. Any moment now she would be able to see who...

'Oh, my *God*!'

April's mouth remained open after her startled exclamation. Any relief she might have felt at finding out it wasn't Max was forgotten as she stared at the approaching stranger. Her heart began to pound, her eyes almost popping out of her head.

For the man was *naked*. Starkers! Wearing nothing but a tan and a pair of wrap-around sunglasses.

Her heartbeat quickened appreciably as her startled gaze skated over his undeniably impressive form. He drew nearer. And nearer. He seemed to be heading right for her uncle's place!

Good grief! Her mother had warned her when she went to live with Uncle Guy in Sydney not to talk to strangers. She imagined *naked* strangers would rate decidedly stronger measures!

Her retreat from the sun-deck was hardly graceful. She lurched backwards, stumbling through the open sliding doorway and falling on to the nearby divan.

Had he realised she had seen him? came the disturbing thought. It was hard to imagine that he hadn't noted her arrival, since she'd had to park the car at the top of the cliff and lug her suitcase down the steep path to the beach-house.

Her face flamed with the possibility that his decision to walk along the beach in the buff was some sort of male ego-trip. True, he was male perfection personified, but surely he wasn't going to come along and introduce himself like *that*!

April's fluster turned to panic. Maybe he was a weirdo, a rapist even. She quickly closed and locked the sliding door then returned to huddle on the divan.

Finally, a type of morbid curiosity drove her to lever herself up on to her knees and peep through the curtained window.

Relief made her head spin for a moment. Her unwanted visitor had stopped, and was now facing out to sea, watching the horizon. Clearly he was unaware of her presence, his whole attitude preoccupied.

She let out a long-held breath but noted with some annoyance that her hands were still trembling, her pulse still racing. Perhaps it was not right to watch him but April could not seem to tear her eyes away, nor stop the erratic thumping of her heart.

Yet there was nothing lewd or obscene about his naked body. In that setting, with the fading light dispatching softly caressing lights, his nudity seemed very natural.

And he *was* beautiful.

Wide bronzed shoulders tapered down to a trim waist and slim hips, well-muscled legs supporting the taut buttocks. It was impossible to see details of his face from that distance but he had a well-shaped head and an attractive thatch of tawny-coloured hair.

April was still staring in spellbound fascination when she saw his shoulders stiffen, his fists suddenly clench at his side. He reminded her of a wild animal, with an animal's tense, unpredictable type of stillness. Any moment he might spring.

So when the stranger's head unexpectedly jerked around to glare up at the house, shock made April bob down. Had he seen her at the window? she flustered. Or was it some sixth sense that made him feel he was being observed?

That must be it, she reasoned more calmly, realising that she couldn't possibly be seen behind the drawn curtains. Rather gingerly she took another peek, comforted to find the man was no longer looking in her direction. In fact he was already turning to walk back the way he had come.

With an ever-increasing compulsion her eyes followed him till he disappeared up the cliff steps into Max's beach-house.

April immediately reached for the phone and dialled, willing that her uncle was at home. He answered on the second ring.

'Guy Richards here.'

'Uncle Guy? It's April. I've arrived safely.'

'And broken the record getting there I would say,' he teased. 'I hope my little Datsun comes back in one piece.'

April laughed. Her uncle was such a dear, insisting on her taking his car, vowing that he rarely used the Datsun anyway, much preferring taxis around the unparkable-in city.

'Had a swim yet?' he asked.

'Well, actually, Uncle, no... You see...'

'Don't tell me you forgot your cossie! Not that you need one up there. No one's to see you if you go skinny-dipping.'

'Well, that's it, you see. There is.'

'There is what?'

'There is someone to see. In fact...' She bit her tongue, stopping short of telling her uncle about her neighbour's state of undress. For a bachelor who'd had as many lady friends as April had fingers and toes, he took his responsibility of looking after his niece with surprising seriousness.

'It seems Max has lent his holiday house to someone,' she informed.

'Really? Who?'

'I don't know, do you?'

'I can't think... Let's see...'

April could hear orchestral music in the background, a sure sign that her uncle was working on one of his articles. She waited patiently.

'Oh, yes.' His sigh carried self-exasperation. 'Max did mention something about letting Hugh Davies use the place while he was away. Sorry, love, I forgot.'

'It's all right,' April hastened to assure him. 'It just gave me a bit of a fright, that's all, seeing a strange man on the beach. By the way, am I supposed to know this Hugh Davies? You sounded as if I should but I could swear I didn't recognise the man.'

And I certainly wouldn't have forgotten this individual, she thought drily.

'Dear heavens, April, surely you remember Hugh? I took you to his exhibition at Max's gallery last year.'

'The sculptor?'

'That's right. You met him, didn't you?'

'I didn't actually speak to him.' April vaguely recalled glancing across a very crowded room at an indifferently dressed man with long brownish hair, a pale complexion and a totally introverted expression. He'd been there, yet not there, clearly uninterested in the gushings of the guests.

'I even bought one of his pieces,' her uncle was saying. 'The one I put on the hall table.'

'Oh, yes...that's right.' It was a curious piece. Quite small, made of grey streaked marble, and shaped into a type of bowl with a curved handle. Around the handle were two rings that could be moved and positioned as one liked, but could not be removed. They'd obviously been carved from the original block of stone, along with the main section, for there were no joins anywhere.

'Well, he must have a friend with him,' April decided aloud. 'The man I saw on the beach is definitely not Hugh Davies.'

'Not everyone vants to be alone,' came her uncle's Greta Garbo impression.

'You would if you'd just spent the entire month of January minding two fourteen-year-old monster brothers twenty-four hours a day.'

Actually, April had been only too glad to do it for her parents. They'd had a difficult year, with her father suffering a nasty bout of shingles and then her mother having a cancer scare. Luckily, the lump in her breast had turned out to be benign, but by Christmas her father had insisted on taking her mother for that overseas holiday they'd always dreamt about and never managed. Of course April's mother had started worrying about leaving the boys, till April had stepped in, promising she would not let the rascals out of her sight.

She hadn't. But it had proved much more wearing than she'd imagined. Worth it, though, when she saw her parents so happy and relaxed on their return.

'You are a noble creature, April Jamieson,' her uncle was saying. 'Almost as noble as a certain long-suffering uncle I know. Now get off this phone before I charge you extra board to cover the bill!'

April grinned, and did as she was told. The truth was that her uncle refused to take any board from her at all. Her parents were not wealthy, and the government student subsidy barely covered the cost of her books, fares, lunches and clothes. But she did repay him by doing most of the cooking and housework.

No sooner had she hung up than her smile faded, to be replaced by a thoughtful look. So the man on the beach was a friend of Hugh Davies, eh? An arty type, no doubt, who probably thought nudity was the way to commune with nature.

April gave herself a mental shake, but she couldn't seem to get the memory of the naked stranger out of her mind. Not that she totally blamed herself. It would have been an odd female who could so easily dismiss such a sight.

Shrugging lightly, she swung away from the phone table and strode across to the small box-freezer, pulling out a steak for her dinner while telling herself quite firmly that she was silly to let her reaction to the man bother her. This wasn't the first male she had found physically attractive in her life. Neither would he be the last.

It was hard to dismiss, though, the fact that he was virtually staying on her doorstep. His presence could prove distracting, and she had come here to have a restful holiday, to use the peace and quiet to refresh her weary spirits for the tough year ahead. She was determined to get the very best pass she could in her final exams, repaying the faith her Uncle Guy had shown in her.

Knowing her ambition to be an economic journalist, he had, after she'd completed the first year of her economics degree with distinctions, approached connections of his at the *Herald*, and they had agreed to take her on when she finished. But then last year...

April squeezed her eyes tightly shut, the memory of what had happened still having the power to upset her. It wasn't that she was still infatuated with Max. She despised the man now. But nothing could wipe out the dismay at her own behaviour, which, while excusable considering her age and Max's undeniable attractions, had still been incredibly naïve. Fancy thinking a thirty-five-year-old playboy would really care about her, particularly a man like Max who was a well-known connoisseur of young women. April knew she had acted like a silly little

fool, both during her stay up here last summer—
and afterwards . . .

She shuddered, recalling only too well that she
had almost destroyed her future in one fell swoop.
How she'd passed her exams last year she would
never know. Her uncle had not said anything when
she'd only scraped passes in all her subjects, but
she had known he was disappointed. And so was
her family.

Just thinking about where her adolescent
emotions had led her hardened April's heart against
her disturbingly attractive neighbour. No way was
she going to let her youthful hormones play havoc
with her this year. No *way*!

She marched into the main bedroom and heaved
her suitcase on to the king-sized water-bed, reaffirming her resolve that men were not on her
agenda this year!

She snapped back the zipper and began lifting
her clothes out on to the bed. But try as she might
thoughts about the man on the beach kept infil-
trating. Who was he? How old was he? What did
he do for a living? Was he . . . ?

April sighed. The stranger's undeniable appeal
seemed to be irrevocably planted in her brain.

And her body . . .

With a rueful shake of her head she tried defusing
her interest with sheer logic. Didn't she realise that
a male as attractive as that would have some female
in tow? If not a wife, then a girlfriend. Maybe
hordes of them! And even if by some miracle he
was single and unattached, who was to say that he
would find her just as attractive?

Why, he probably likes tall, willowy blondes, she decided, not petite brunettes!

Not that colouring and size were the only factors that turned some men off, she acknowledged with feeling as Max's cruel words of a year ago catapulted into her mind.

'You must be jesting, April. A *virgin* ... At *nineteen*?' He had managed to look disbelieving and bored at one and the same time. 'Look, darling, initiations were never my scene. I think you'd better run along, but by all means come back after the big event, then I'll be only too willing.'

April cringed as she remembered Max's taunts. She cringed even more as she thought again of her immature reaction at the time.

She had gone back to university, defiantly determined to become the sort of sophisticated woman Max would be interested in. She had even gone on the Pill. Another of his caustic suggestions.

Thank the lord that despite engaging in constant partying and socialising, and having countless offers from some of the best-looking guys on the campus, when it came down to the nitty gritty she had kept running a mile.

It had finally dawned on her that she was acting like a little fool, and that Max was a thirty-five-year-old creep!

April had decided then and there that her first sexual experience was going to be something special, with someone special. She wanted it to be part of a true romance, a love-affair where she was carried away with passion.

Passion.

April turned her head to stare at the window. The thought insinuated into her mind that with the man on the beach she could feel passion...

Her frown was swift and dark. This was getting ridiculous, she thought irritably.

With quick angry movements she began unpacking her suitcase. When she pulled out her skimpy red bikini she gave the sexy garment an honest appraisal then stuffed it back in the suitcase, drawing out instead a sensible black *maillot*. Now that was more like it!

When she finished unpacking, April hurried around, opening windows, turning on lights and generally making a lot of noise. She turned the radio up full blast. One thing was for sure. She was going to make certain her neighbour, or neighbours, were well acquainted with her arrival, and would hopefully put some clothes on in future.

Night came slowly, February still being cursed with daylight saving. Tired from the long drive, April retired early, though she found it hard to get used to her uncle's water-bed. On other visits she had slept on the convertible divan. But gradually weariness took hold of her body, the sensations of disturbing movement slowly changing to soothing, lulling rocking. As April slipped over that edge from semi-consciousness to oblivion, one final thought infiltrated.

His eyes would be blue...

CHAPTER TWO

When April awoke the next morning, she was disorientated for a few seconds, wondering why she was in a strange bed. Realisation of where she was and what had happened the previous afternoon brought a nervous flutter. Would she run into her interesting neighbour today? And, perhaps more to the point, would he have some clothes on?

She was to have her answers the second she stepped outside for her morning jog.

Yes. To both questions.

He was lying low in the sand, not far from where the stone steps led up the cliff to Max's beach-house. April might have missed him except for a slash of royal blue in the middle of his tanned length.

At least I succeeded in getting him to wear a swimming-costume, she thought, trying hard to control an irritating surge of adrenalin.

Damn it all! This was not what she had in mind for her holiday. She'd been looking forward to quiet swims, relaxing sunbathing, hours of reading and music, all by herself. It was annoying to have to worry about sharing the small beach, particularly with this macho male who kept bombarding her thoughts and disturbing her equilibrium.

She pulled her bright pink T-shirt well down over her black costume and set off across the sand, reaffirming her resolve not to encourage any untoward developments. All she had to do was make some innocuous greeting when he saw her and keep on running. Nothing hard about that.

The morning breeze was unexpectedly sharp, causing goose-bumps to spring up on her arms. Shivering, she hurried down to the firmer sand at the water's edge and broke into a light jog. As she drew closer to his outstretched form her heart began to pound in unison with her feet. Any minute now he would become aware of her.

But he didn't!

Or didn't seem to.

He just lay there, staring upwards, the opaque sunglasses firmly in place. If he noticed her going by he certainly gave no indication of it. Neither did he acknowledge her presence when she turned and went by again.

It was an oddly peeved April who returned to her uncle's beach-house a few minutes later.

'Well!' she exclaimed, dropping down on the divan. 'How do you like that? Not even so much as a twitch. No recognition whatsoever.'

It took all of an hour and three cups of coffee for April to get over the feeling she had been well and truly snubbed.

But another explanation of events finally dawned on her. He was asleep! That was it. Out like a light. She could imagine how warm and comfortable it was nestled low in the sand, out of the wind.

With the third, nearly empty mug cradled in her hands April found herself standing at the window, watching him again. Somehow her decision not to let this man's presence intrude into her life had been forgotten.

Shortly he got up, stretched, then put himself through the most rigorous workout of exercises April had ever seen. It was awe-inspiring. So many push-ups! Then he strolled down to swim lazily in the almost waveless water.

Watching him exercise had made her feel hot and sticky but April was loath to join her neighbour in the water. Yet the longer she stayed in the house pretending to herself she was not watching him, the more unsettled she became.

It was all so silly, the way she was building him into a mental fantasy. OK, so he didn't appear to have a female—wife or girlfriend—with him. But so what? Up close he was probably not so good-looking. He was also probably as thick as a brick. Unintelligent men always bored April to tears, no matter how handsome they were.

Before she could think better of it, April stripped off her T-shirt and picked up a towel, fully intending to go for a swim, and, if the situation arose, to casually introduce herself. But by the time she covered the distance between her uncle's beach-house and the water, the man had left the water and was towelling himself down. And once again he seemed to be deliberately ignoring her, for he didn't look up or give any indication of her approach.

Exasperation made her decide to go right up to him and say something. Otherwise she would be nervy and self-conscious every time she came down for a swim. Even now, as she walked towards him, her stomach was full of butterflies.

She was almost on top of him when suddenly his head jerked upwards to face her. The cold, hard glare from behind those opaque shields would have unnerved the most confident female.

April froze. Then bristled. How she detested those sunglasses! The type that allowed the wearer to see out but no one to see in, the type so often worn by male movie stars.

But there again, she realised sinkingly, this fellow *was* movie star material. While not classically handsome, he was still very attractively male with a strong nose, a wide firm mouth and aggressive chin. Even with his hair wet and slicked back, he looked good.

The strain of his icy stare finally got the better of her. 'Hello, there,' she chirped. 'Been in for a swim, I see. Is the water cold?'

'Yes. Quite cold.' His voice would have been rich and deep if he hadn't clipped his words short in barely held irritation.

April swallowed and went on bravely. 'My name's April Jamieson,' she said, though making no attempt to hold out her hand. 'I'm staying at the other beach-house.'

'So I gathered,' he said without even looking up. He just kept on towelling his legs dry. 'One would have had to have been deaf to have missed your arrival last night.'

Such unexpected sarcasm took April aback for a second, but perhaps she *had* overdone things last night. Still, it was a comfort to know he didn't

realise she had arrived in time to see his nude stroll.
'Yes, it took me all day to drive up from Sydney,'
she rattled on brightly. 'This is my uncle's place.
I'm living with him, you see, while I'm——'

'Really, Miss Jamieson, I——'

'Oh, do call me April,' she cut in carelessly.

'April,' he ground out through clenched teeth.
'Look, if you don't mind I'd rather not hear about
your living arrangements. All I want is to be left
alone.'

There was a limit to April's good-natured
tolerance, a line over which she would not allow
others to cross. This excuse for a person had just
put his big male foot over it. Her chin lifted defiantly, her nostrils flaring. 'Suits me,' she returned
coldly. 'Who would want to talk to someone as rude
as you anyway?' And with that she whirled round
and began to stride away, her angry feet stamping
into the sand.

'Miss Jamieson...April! Stop!' he shouted after
her.

She kept on going.

'Please?' he added.

She ground to a reluctant halt. 'What?' she
demanded, her face still flaming with fury and self-
reproach. She should have known better than to
even speak to such an individual. There was not
one overly good-looking male of her acquaintance
who wasn't insufferably arrogant and opinionated.

He lifted his shoulders in a careless shrug. The
morning rays glinted on his now drying, sun-
streaked hair. 'What can I say? That *was* unforgiv-
ably rude of me.' His smile was wry, and damnably

attractive. 'Would you accept an apology, humbly delivered?'

Humbly delivered, my eye, she thought, and remained mutinously silent.

'Come back and sit down,' his voice beckoned with that seductive quality she just knew it could possess.

Despite still feeling annoyed, she began to walk slowly back. He settled down where he was and patted the spot beside him. 'Come on,' he said, glancing up at her. 'Sit down. The sand's pleasantly warm.'

'Oh ... All right.'

This friendly about-face dissolved the last of April's anger. Perhaps this chap was the exception to the rule. She did as he asked, sinking down into the sand with a winning smile on her previously scowling face.

Nevertheless, it didn't take her long to realise that she was wasting her smiles. The man beside her didn't respond in kind or give her a second look. He hunched forward, knees raised, arms wrapped around shins, and stared blankly out to sea. She found his indifference quite hurtful.

'I haven't been well,' he said simply, as though that excused everything.

April's eyes flicked over the rippling muscles, the healthy glowing skin. 'You certainly look well,' she voiced without thinking. Then flushed.

He didn't seem to notice. 'Really?' The word had the oddest inflexion. It was vaguely sceptical.

There was a moment's awkward silence.

'Max told me that Guy Richards owns the other beach-house,' he finally said, still not looking at her. 'I've met him, I recall. He's an art critic.'

'Uncle Guy does do some art reviews,' she explained, just managing to hide her uncustomary pique, 'but I wouldn't call him an art critic. He's a freelance journalist and writes up all sorts of things, from sport to cooking competitions. He did do an article on your friend though.'

He turned his head towards her, a frown forming wrinkles on his high, wide forehead. 'My what?'

'Your friend,' she repeated. 'Hugh Davies...'

The frown deepened. April longed for him to take off the glasses so she could see what he was thinking.

'But I...' He hesitated, cocking his head to one side in obvious puzzlement. 'What makes you say that?'

She blinked her surprise. 'Well, I thought... Uncle Guy said... I mean... You *are* a friend of Hugh Davies, aren't you?'

Suddenly the frown dissolved and he laughed. The sound had a disturbingly mocking edge. 'Sometimes.'

'Isn't he staying here, then?' she persisted, feeling totally confused now.

'Oh, yes,' he agreed. 'Hugh and I go everywhere together. We're old, old friends.'

'I see,' she murmured, not seeing at all. 'Are you both sculptors?'

'Yes and no.'

She stared at him. 'What does that mean?'

He smiled. Or at least his mouth did. April felt certain that, even if she could see his eyes, they would not be joining in. 'Never mind. Yes, I'm a sculptor too. Or, at least, I might be, some day soon...' His lips compressed into an impatient line and finally the penny dropped for April. He was obviously a protégé of Hugh Davies, still learning his craft, still tortured with doubts about his own ability. Her uncle had many aspiring artist friends and they were all like that. Torn, intense, full of insecurities. Till success came. Then they were simply arrogant.

A thought struck. At least Hugh Davies had not seemed arrogant. April slid a surreptitious look at her companion. It was unlikely that *this* individual would be similarly unaffected, she decided, if he ever hit the big scene. She could imagine it now. Women dripping all over him, flattering him, propositioning him...

His face half turned towards her and her gaze drifted from his stubborn-looking mouth to the sunglases... Darn, but she wished he'd take those infernal things off! Even up close they were complete blinds.

'Tell me, April, what do you think of Hugh's work?' he enquired. 'Or haven't you seen any of it?'

'I went to one of his exhibitions once,' she confessed. 'He's obviously very good, and I love that streaky marble he uses, but I have to admit I found him a trifle off-putting.'

'You've *met* Hugh?' The question carried so much astonishment that April felt peeved. Was it so unlikely that a mere mortal had met such a rising star?

'Not actually,' she tossed off. 'But he was there, drifting reluctantly from group to group and looking as if he wished everyone would disappear.'

His laughter was dry. 'That sounds familiar. Antisocial through and through. One thing intrigues me, though. When we met just now you automatically assumed I wasn't Hugh. Yet I've been told we could be mistaken for one another.'

It was April's turn to laugh. 'How ridiculous! You don't look anything alike. Why he's...he's... Well, he's... And you're...'

April floundered. She was not going to boost this man's ego by saying he was God's gift to women whereas Hugh Davies was...well... She frowned, realising that she couldn't really recall what Hugh Davies looked like in any detail. All her attention had been focused on Max that night. Nevertheless...

'I can assure you that no one would mistake you for your friend,' she went on with conviction. 'For one thing you're bigger. And your hair's a different colour. Fairer.'

'Oh?' His eyebrows lifted up over the rim of the sunglasses and he ran an absent hand through his hair. It was fully dry now, the blond streaks lightening it to its attractive tawny colour.

'What *is* your name, by the way?' April asked.

'My name? Oh—er—Harold... Harold Chambers.' His lips curved slowly back into an odd smile. 'But you can call me Harry.'

Harry? He was called *Harry*? It just showed you, April thought ruefully, that appearances could be deceiving. There she was thinking he'd be called something forceful like Blake or Leon. Even Hugh was better than Harry!

'OK,' she said with a sigh. What did it matter what he was named or what she called him? She followed her companion's idea and wrapped her arms around bent knees. It was a surprisingly comfortable position. And the sun was warming up, beating down on her head and shoulders with a drugging heat.

'So you quite liked Hugh's work, did you?' he persisted.

'His smaller pieces were particularly nice,' she said.

'*Nice*? What does nice mean, for God's sake?' he said so sharply that April's mouth dropped open. Her surprise quickly became resentment. Who did he think he was, talking to her like that?

'It means *nice*!' she retorted. 'Like in pleasing to the eye. I happen to like the word nice. It's better than those pseudo-intellectual adjectives art people come up with. When I say his smaller pieces are nice that's meant as a positive, complimentary statement.'

'Hmm.' Harry looked as thoughtful as he could with sunglasses on. He stroked his chin and turned to look at her. 'Why the smaller pieces especially?'

She shrugged. 'I don't know. I guess it's a pleasant change to find a sculptor who creates art that can be picked up and admired, and can be placed in the ordinary home. Modern sculpture is usually so unwieldy.'

'Unwieldy,' he repeated slowly.

'Yes. You know, only fit for massive concrete courtyards and such. What good are they to a small collector who lives in a two-room flat? Look, I know you're a sculptor too, but can I be frank?' She was rather enjoying herself, giving vent to her plebeian ideas. She firmly pushed aside the notion that she might be acting like a woman scorned.

His mouth twitched in one corner. 'I get the impression you always would be.'

She gave an irritable sigh. 'I just wish people would be more honest about art and stop following the so-called experts' opinions like sheep. I don't mean to offend you——' Oh, yes, you do, April Jamieson, her conscience inserted '—but I find most sculpture a bit of a con. Pieces of metal thrown together then given some airy-fairy title like ''Survival''. People come along and rave over it and they use words like dimension and perspective, but no ordinary person has a clue what they're talking about.'

She waited for him to come back at her but he didn't. He just sat there, silently nodding. It rather took all the wind out of April's sails.

'From what I heard,' he said slowly, 'some of the international critics didn't overly like those smaller pieces you mentioned.'

'See what I mean? What would they know? If you ask me, Hugh Davies would do well to stick to making smaller pieces. Uncle Guy bought one and he's got excellent taste.'

'Which one?'

'The oddly shaped bowl with the curved handle and the two rings. Fascinating, I find it.'

'Fascinating?'

'Yes. Occasionally when I go past it I slip the rings into another position and it makes it look entirely different.'

'You mean it gains a different perspective,' he teased.

April couldn't keep up her attack. She burst out laughing and so did he. But she stopped abruptly when she found herself staring at his mouth and wondering what it would be like to be kissed by it. It perturbed her how much she wanted this man to fancy her, particularly since it was clear that he did not.

'Hugh!'

They both spun round on their bottoms at the sound of the loud shout. A giant of a man was standing on Max's concrete balcony. He was totally bald and reminded April of one of the henchmen from a James Bond movie.

'Breakfast's ready,' the voice grated out. 'Come on, Hugh. Hurry up or the steak'll be cold.'

'Coming.'

April stared as the man next to her stood up. 'But... but...' she squeaked. 'Is that man calling to *you*?'

He looked back down at her and the sudden silence was electric. 'Afraid so,' he said at last. 'Well, April? I'm waiting for you to tear strips off me. Don't disappoint me.'

April gaped up at him. The realisation that this actually was Hugh Davies looking down at her, Hugh Davies she'd been talking to, Hugh Davies who had drawn her into making such outrageous statements, made her blush furiously. She supposed someone must have pointed out the wrong man to her at the exhibition.

'You should have told me,' she blurted out. 'Oh, God, I've never felt so embarrassed in all my life!'

'Embarrassed? *You*?' His laughter was mocking. 'There's not an embarrassed bone in your body, April Jamieson! Besides, you've only got yourself to blame. You kept insisting that there was no way I could be mistaken for Hugh Davies.' He chuckled. 'Come on.' He held out a conciliatory hand to help her up.

April groaned, put her hand into his solid palm and levered herself up on to her feet. 'But you said your name was Harry,' she accused.

'A little white lie. That's Harry.' Hugh nodded towards the man who'd called out.

She could feel the heat of his hand seeping into her own. Her blood began to race, her skin to tingle. 'That wasn't nice,' she muttered.

His smile was oddly cynical. 'I don't claim to be nice. Anyway, at least I got an honest criticism. You've no idea how hard that is to come by.'

'For Pete's sake, Hugh,' came the impatient bark from the beach-house. 'Shake a leg, will you?'

'Fancy some breakfast?' he asked, and dropped her hand. April felt instantly chilled.

She glanced up at the big man on the balcony. His face was grim, his whole bearing formidable.

'Er—no, I don't think so. Your friend looks...um...'

'Don't worry about Harry. He's not too keen on women but his bark is worse than his bite.'

'Another time maybe,' she murmured.

'Fair enough. Well, it's been interesting talking to you, April. Most...enlightening.'

Enlightening.

April thought about that word as she wandered back along the beach. She supposed that by enlightening he meant he'd gleaned a frank opinion of his sculpture, even if it was inspired more by pique than the need to be honest. She wished she felt similarly enlightened about why she kept being attracted to the wrong men. The only consolation was that Hugh was quite a bit younger than Max. Late twenties, she guessed. How ironic, though, that with Max she hadn't been able to get him to keep his hands and eyes off her body. Yet with Hugh she could hardly get him to look at her at all!

She was back at the beach-house before the memory hit her. And it quite took her breath away.

It had been Max who had pointed out the sculptor to her at the exhibition. And Max would not have been mistaken.

The situation was so puzzling, so perplexing that she just had to telephone her uncle again.

'So soon, April?' Guy joked.

'I've just run into Hugh Davies,' she said straight away.

'Yes?'

'Could you tell me what he looks like?'

There was a moment's silence before he came back on the line, sounding worried. 'Is this some sort of joke, April?'

'No, of course not,' she said hurriedly. 'It's just that he doesn't look the same. He's...different from the man I saw at the exhibition. Do me a favour and describe him for me.'

'Really, April!'

'Please...'

He sighed. 'OK. Reasonably tall, very lean, brownish hair, attractive but anaemic-looking. Interesting eyes. Deep-set, bluish grey. Won't make the world's ten best dressed this year,' he finished with a laugh.

'That's not him,' she said bluntly.

'Not him? What do you mean, not him? Of course it's him, I've met him more than once.'

'I mean that's not the man on the beach, claiming he's Hugh Davies.' April shivered. Fear rippled down her spine.

'April, are you sure?'

'Yes...' Her voice was barely a whisper.

'Look, April, hang up and lock the door. God knows what's going on but I'll ring Max's gallery and speak to his assistant. Then I'll ring you back. If you're still worried then you'd better come home, OK?'

April paced the floor, waiting breathlessly for him to call back. She wanted to believe that the man on the beach had been a genuine individual, but strange things happened in this world. There were all sorts of confidence tricksters in operation, most of them handsome men preying on vulnerable women. She prayed that was not the case this time.

When the phone rang she snatched up the receiver. 'Uncle Guy?'

'Breathe easy, love. It is Hugh Davies. Seems he was in a car accident soon after the exhibition. No life-threatening injuries but he does look different, I gather. His jaw was broken and had to be re-wired, for one thing. And it seems he's employed some sort of trainer chap to get him fit and healthy for more surgery. Apparently he's built his body up considerably, which makes him look bigger and taller. Would that explain the changes?'

April struggled to take in the surprising news. Accident, hospital, surgery... But it did all fit, she supposed, particularly the bit about the trainer. That had to be the bruiser on the balcony.

'Well, yes, I guess so...' Her mind flew to his hair colour till she remembered that weeks in the sun could have bleached it at the same time as it had turned his previously pale skin into bronze. And yet...

'Oh, and Max's secretary says he's become a pain to deal with, not the quiet self-contained Hugh of old. But I can understand that. Hell, it can't be easy having to put your creative urges on hold. It's all very well for doctors to say that something is only temporary. If it were me I'd be damn worried, I can tell you.'

'What do you mean?' April asked. 'Is there something wrong with his hands?'

'Didn't I say? No, it's not his hands. It's his eyes. They were damaged in the accident. He's temporarily blind.'

CHAPTER THREE

APRIL'S mouth dropped open. She blinked a few times. 'Blind?' she repeated, shock rippling through her. 'But he can't be! I mean, he...he...' Her voice trailed away as the truth of her uncle's news sank in. It explained so much. The impenetrable glasses; his failing to notice her jog along the beach; his avoidance of looking at her; that confusing 'yes and no' comment about being a sculptor.

'Oh, Uncle Guy, how awful for him,' she groaned. To be suddenly locked in a world of dark helplessness would be dreadful at any time. For a man like Hugh it would be utter torture.

'Yes. Very frustrating, I would imagine. But at least he should recover. Eventually.'

Eventually... What a ghastly word for Hugh to come to terms with! Even in the short while she had known him April sensed that patience was not one of his virtues. As for living without his sculpting... She recalled how in her uncle's article Hugh had come over as a loner, a man who lived and breathed his art, claiming he was lost when not working.

'I have to go, April. There's someone at the door. Have a nice time, and give my best wishes to Hugh, will you? I gather he's to have an operation in the not too distant future.'

'All right. Will do.'

An hour later, April was seated at the small kitchen counter, her toast going cold in front of her, her mind still preoccupied with the startling news.

Blind.

Poor Hugh. What he must have gone through—was *still* going through. Her heart turned over as sympathy welled up again inside her. Thank God it wasn't going to be permanent. At least... A momentary doubt sliced through her, making her feel almost ill. Surely the doctors wouldn't give him false hope, would they?

April gave herself a mental shake. She refused to think like that, refused to be pessimistic. Hugh was going to get his sight back. He *was*! The alternative didn't bear thinking about.

But a frown came to her face as she wondered why he hadn't told her about his blindness, why he... Oh, of course, she thought, and nodded resignedly. He wouldn't want pity. Not a man like him.

Yes, April felt very sorry for Hugh. Very sorry indeed. And she felt ashamed of herself for the way she'd been trying to attract his attention. Her romantic fantasies seemed juvenile and selfish in the light of the great personal trial Hugh was facing. The last thing he needed was some female throwing herself at his head. A friend he might welcome. Nothing more.

April sighed. But then shrugged. Be honest, she lectured herself. Isn't that all *you* want at this time in your life? Aren't you just a little relieved that something has come along to put a halt to those rapidly escalating feelings of yours?

'Too right!' she pronounced aloud, and stood up to make herself some fresh toast.

The rest of the day promised to be hot, a perfect day for swimming. And the cove was made for swimming. The reef that stretched across between the rocky headlands broke the waves and the water inside held only the barest of swells. April had always preferred it to the open surf which she found tiresome and inevitably crowded. No one came to this place.

After breakfast April went straight from the house into the water, not intending at that point to venture down Hugh's end of the beach. She could appreciate that most of the time he probably did want privacy, but she believed that being alone all the time was not healthy for the mind. Perhaps she would go along and talk to him later. After his initial aloofness he had seemed to appreciate her company.

The water was cold at first, but she soon got used to it. And when she tired of stroking up and down she turned over and lay on her back. Closing her eyes, she stretched out her arms and floated, the warm rays beating down on her cooled body. It was infinitely relaxing and she must have stayed that way for longer than she realised, for when she lifted her head it was a shock to find that she had drifted way down the other end.

'Hey, April!' came a shout across the water. 'Harry said you should watch that rip. You might get carried on to the rocks.'

It was Hugh, standing at the water's edge, his hands cupped around his mouth. April waved and shouted that she was OK, but when she began to tread water she suddenly felt the dangerous pull around her ankles.

Swallowing her panic, she started heading towards the beach, all the time fighting against the treacherous undertow. It was slow going and by the time she made dry land she was exhausted. She dragged herself up on to the sand, her lungs bursting, her breath gasping.

'April?' Hugh was instantly there, reaching down and pulling her bedraggled wet form up against his warm but equally scantily clad body. 'Are you all right? April? Say something!'

'I'm fine,' she expelled shakily, her skin breaking into goose-bumps as he rubbed her arms up and down.

'You're terribly cold.'

Her teeth began to chatter. But there was nothing cold about the sensations charging through her at Hugh's touch. And she had thought sympathy for his condition would dampen the sexual attraction she felt for him! Evidence to the contrary made her heart turn over with dismay.

'You silly girl,' he reproached. 'Look, my towel's over here.' He guided her across the sand, unerringly making for the brightly coloured towel lying in the sand. He picked it up and wrapped it around her shoulders, then flicked the wet strands of hair out of her eyes and smoothed them behind her ears. All she could do was stare up at him, her mouth open.

'But I thought you were blind?' she blurted out.

He stiffened, his jaw clenching tight, the muscles twitching along the base of his cheeks. 'So you've found out about that, have you? Pity. I was rather enjoying your refreshing lack of sympathy.'

'But...but you saw this towel on the sand just now,' she accused. 'I'm sure you did.'

'In a fashion,' he conceded curtly. 'I can recognise light and dark to a degree, and bright colours. In the sunshine here I can just make out your vague outline. Your very short outline, might I add.'

It was a sore point with her—her height. Her twin brothers had shot up past her at age eleven. And never ceased to tease her about it. For a second she lost any urge to act sympathetically. 'I'm almost five feet four!' she declared.

His mouth pulled back into a wry smile. 'Who do you think you're kidding, sweetheart? I'm a sculptor. I felt you.'

She blushed at the memory of his hands in her hair. 'OK, so I'm only five two and a bit. Just because you're a giant!'

He gave a dry laugh. 'Five eleven—*and three quarters*—is hardly a giant. But I'm glad to see my blindness is not warranting any special treatment. I should have known it wouldn't with you.' He laughed again, and this time the sound had lost its cutting edge. 'You know, April, I think you're good for me. You amuse me. I haven't found much to laugh at lately.'

'Want to hire me as your court jester?' she suggested cheekily.

'Are you expensive?'

'Frightfully.'

'Too bad. I was hoping you'd donate your time for nothing as a charitable gesture. I'll have to count my pennies now that I can't...' The ready smile faded, a black cloud sweeping across his face. 'Good God, what am I doing? Making stupid damned jokes about it when for all I know I might never see again, might never——'

He broke off and slammed heavily down on to the sand, taking up the same position as before, knees bent, arms wrapped around shins. But where then he had seemed reasonably relaxed, now he was a taut bundle of anguish and anger. 'For heaven's sake, go!' he threw up at her. 'I'm not fit company for anyone at the moment.'

April ached to put her arms around him, to hug him and tell him everything would be all right. But she knew he would hate that, would see it as a sign of pity. 'What a grouch you are, Hugh,' she said with feigned intolerance. 'But you don't frighten me. I have two brothers who make your bad temper look like kindergarten playtime.' She plopped down on the sand beside him. 'I have no intention of going till I find out exactly what's wrong with your eyes. I was talking to Uncle Guy on the phone and he told me you'd had some sort of accident, and that an operation can fix you up, but that's all I know.'

'And, being a typical female,' Hugh snarled, 'you want to know all the gruesome details!'

'But of course.' She laughed.

'Tough. I don't like to talk about it.'

'Can't you at least tell me when the operation's scheduled? And where?' she persisted.

'Why do you want to know?' he asked suspiciously.

She shrugged before she remembered he couldn't see the gesture. 'Wouldn't you like visitors?'

'Not particularly.'

'Tough. I think I'll come anyway.'

She could see he was startled. 'Why would you want to do that? We hardly know each other.'

April fell silent. He was right, of course. From his point of view, they were only mild acquaintances of very brief duration. He wasn't to know that already she was being carried along by a tide of feeling for him too strong to deny. Even sitting here next to him was an insidiously pleasurable experience. She could watch him, let her eyes feast upon his lovely male body without the chance of being caught.

'How old are you, anyway?' he asked abruptly. 'Seventeen? Eighteen? Harry said you were young. You sound young.'

People had even mistaken her for sixteen. It was her stupid height, she knew. Thank the lord she had well-developed breasts. 'I'm twenty,' she announced firmly.

'Twenty,' he repeated, shaking his head and sounding as if twenty were still a baby.

'Twenty's not so young.' Her voice was defensive. 'I'll be twenty-one soon.' When he made no comment she said, 'Well? How old are *you*?'

'Old . . . very old.'

'You don't look old.'

'Ah, yes, but there are two kinds of old. The one I'm talking about is in here——' he pointed to his head '—and here.' The finger indicated his heart.

Suddenly he looked so bleak. It moved her unbearably.

'Tell me more about yourself,' he insisted.

She sat back on the sand and sighed. She would rather have talked about him. He still hadn't told her anything about his blindness. Or how old he really was. 'What would you like to know?' she asked.

'Hair colour?'

'Black.'

'Eyes?'

'Blue.'

'Job?'

'University student. Sydney. Last year economics degree.'

He whistled. 'Smart too, eh?'

'What do you mean, smart too?'

'Smart as well as beautiful.'

She was thankful he couldn't see her blush. 'I wouldn't call myself beautiful. Anyway, I thought you could only see a vague outline.'

He laughed. 'Harry has twenty-twenty vision and he says you're a looker.'

Compliments always flustered her. 'I think your Harry's an exaggerater.'

'Could be, April. Could be…' He turned his head slightly towards her. 'He seemed to think you might fancy me?'

'*Fancy* you?' April repeated, her throat constricting.

'Yes. Apparently I qualify as a ladies' man now that I boast a few muscles and a tan. Not to mention my sexy sun-streaked hair,' he added sarcastically. His mouth pulled back into a startlingly bitter grimace. 'Perhaps if I'd had them a few months ago, my darling fiancée wouldn't have been so swift to decamp after the accident.'

April struggled to handle a whole host of emotions. Not the least of which was dismay at finding out Hugh had been recently engaged. Yet hadn't she known there would be a woman somewhere? And while his relationship with this un-named woman was apparently over, his feelings for her obviously were not.

'Well, April?' he prodded caustically. 'Is Harry right? Do my newly acquired superficial attractions appeal to your adolescent eye?'

April bristled. It was the second time Hugh had sounded condescending about her age. Clearly he thought that any female who'd just left their teenage years couldn't have a sensible thought in their silly, shallow, empty heads. She could see that even if he weren't blind, even if he hadn't still been hurting over a broken engagement, such an attitude ruined any hope of a relationship between them.

This last realisation hurt far more deeply than she had been prepared for, her dented pride and heart making her answer with an offhand flippancy. 'You don't have to worry about me on that score, Hugh.' She laughed far too brightly. 'If there's one thing a university is full of it's good-looking, superficial males. The only thing they think about is sex, sex, sex! It really gets to be a bore after a while. That's why I came up here to this place. To get away from that sort of thing for a while.'

For a few elongated seconds he sat in grim silence.

April was aware that, in her anxiety to sound unaffected and sophisticated, she had overdone it, actually sounding like the immature flip he obviously thought her to be. She regretted it immediately, but the damage had been done. When Hugh next spoke his voice held a sardonic note.

'It sounds as if nothing's changed since my days at university. The favourite game then was musical beds.'

'Not everyone is like that,' she muttered irritably.

'No?' he scoffed. 'I dare say there's the odd exception, but somehow I don't think that would be you, April, my love. You don't sound like the prim and proper type.'

'There's a vast range between being prim and proper and promiscuous,' she pointed out indignantly.

'Is there? I doubt that these days. Still, I guess you can't put an old head on young shoulders.'

'Will you stop talking like Methuselah?' she said sharply. 'Good grief, you couldn't be older than twenty-seven or -eight at the most.'

'Well, well! I must congratulate Harry on his exercise programme. I'm thirty-four.'

She was shocked. That meant he was only one year younger than Max. Good grief, why was she always attracted to older men? 'You don't *look* that old,' she argued futilely.

'Sceptical? Let's see, I left school at eighteen, spent three years at Sydney University, four years in London, one in New York, another two in Italy, then it took me six years of solid work getting ready for that exhibition. How are you at maths?'

'It happens to be my second-best subject,' she retorted, irked that Hugh seemed hell-bent on making their age-gap seem wider than it was! 'Thirty-four, eh?' she tossed off with obvious exasperation. 'Oh, well, only twenty-six more years and you'll be getting the pension. How time flies!'

His laughter was genuine this time. 'I do sound like an old pain, don't I? Can I claim mental stress as the excuse?'

'You can claim it,' she countered, 'but I won't believe it. I think you're just jealous!'

'Jealous?' He appeared genuinely astonished.

'Yes. Jealous! You've lost the art of having fun, but you don't like others to have it.'

'And you think leaping into bed with every Tom, Dick and Harry is fun? Haven't you ever stopped to think of the possible consequences?'

'Oh, don't be such an old fuddy-duddy,' she declared, frustrated at having been so misunderstood.

'A *fuddy-duddy*?'

'Yes. A fuddy-duddy!'

He burst out into rollicking laughter.

'What's the big joke?'

April's head jerked up to see Harry looming over them, his bulk blocking out the sun. A chill invaded her.

'April thinks I'm an old fuddy-duddy.' Hugh chuckled.

Harry gave her a sharp, suspicious look. It sent shivers up her spine. 'Time for your massage,' he growled.

'OK.' Hugh levered himself up on to muscular legs. April stood up too, knowing that she had just been expertly dismissed by the watch-dog.

'Oh, Harry, this is April Jamieson, Guy Richards' niece, the chap who owns the other beach-house.'

'Miss Jamieson.' Harry nodded coldly.

'April, meet Harry Chambers, fellow sculptor, truck driver, nurse, gym instructor, chauffeur, and my all-time best mate.'

April was taken aback, by Hugh's words and the flash of true warmth that leapt into Harry's world-weary eyes, a pleasure that died when he glanced back at her. 'You forgot to mention ex-con.'

Hugh's mouth thinned. 'I didn't forget, Harry, but that's over now.'

'I just like to have it all out in the open,' Harry persisted grimly, 'and then people don't get any nasty surprises later on. Do you want to know what I was in there for, girlie?'

'Harry...' Hugh warned.

'I don't mind knowing,' April said, 'if you don't mind telling me.'

'Grand larceny. Then escaping lawful custody. Served eleven years.'

There was a charged silence.

April kept her eyes steady, feeling suddenly sorry for the big, brusque man with the hard, wary eyes.

'As Hugh said, Harry——' her voice was low and gentle '—you've paid your debt to society...' She held out her hand. 'And any friend of Hugh's is a friend of mine.'

Harry's expression betrayed a grudging surprise but he shook hands. 'Yeah, well, some people don't look at it that way.' He dropped her hand, turned and stalked off. 'Mornin' tea's ready if you want some, girlie,' he growled over his shoulder.

Hugh reached for and found her shoulder. He leant close. 'That was sweet, April. Really sweet. And, believe me, there's no harm in Harry.'

April was no longer thinking about Harry. Her mind was solely concentrated on the touch of Hugh's hand and the warm whisper of his breath on her hair.

'Well, come on ... girlie,' Hugh said teasingly, his fingers finally slipping off her shoulder. 'Help me find my suntan lotion. It's here somewhere.'

'Really!' she huffed, relieved that he had moved away. 'I thought you didn't want any special treatment! You've been getting around pretty well all by yourself and now you can't find a little itty-bitty tube.' The light banter hid a still thudding heart.

'That was before I had a female around to wait on me,' he countered. 'Harry makes me fend for myself. Found it? Good. Take my hand and lead me home.'

Leading him home proved quite an experience, particularly when he insisted on more solid support up the steep steps that had been cut into the cliff-face. They were still damp, he said. He slipped an arm around her waist and the side of her breast brushed up against his ribs.

Immediately a rush of heat invaded her body and she was quick to move away from him as soon as they reached the overhead balcony. The intensity of her response to a mere accidental contact was disturbing.

Harry opened the door for them and led Hugh to a stool at the vast breakfast bar. Max's house was a far cry from her uncle's simple wooden dwelling. This was spacious luxury, made of concrete and glass, with stark leather furniture and all mod cons. She had been very impressed last year when Max had invited her inside. Now she saw it for what it was. An expensive, characterless building reflecting the taste of an expensive, characterless man.

'Want a biscuit?' came the blunt question as Harry plonked two mugs of tea on the marble counter.

'No, thanks,' she murmured.

Hugh patted the stool next to his. 'Sit here next to me, April, and tell me some more about yourself. First of all, why are you living with your uncle? Where's your family?'

'They live in Nyngan.'

'Aah, a country girl. You're from the country, aren't you, Harry?'

Harry grunted.

'And this is your last year at university? What are you going to do when you leave?'

She took a sip of the tea. 'I have a job lined up at the *Herald*, as a cadet journalist in the business section.'

'That's a bit serious for a girl like you, isn't it?'

Again, Hugh's patronising tone rubbed April up the wrong way. 'I don't think so,' she said sharply.

'You don't have to get all uppity!'

'Then don't talk down to me. You sound just like my father.'

'Well, I'm nearly old enough to *be* your father, aren't I?' he said predictably. 'So tell us, April, how long will you be staying up here?'

'Two weeks.'

'Exactly the time I've got left before I have to go back to Sydney for my operation. I think we could just about stand her for two weeks, don't you, Harry?'

The big man busying himself in the well-appointed kitchen issued another grunt along with a guarded glance.

April groaned silently. Two weeks. Two long weeks of a sort of masochistic torture, being near this devastatingly sexy man and having him treat her like a naughty adolescent. And, in the background, his henchman, watching her every move.

'I couldn't last two weeks without knowing what happened to your eyes,' she said defiantly.

Hugh chuckled. 'Fair enough. Simply put, I was in a car accident. A collision at an intersection... The windscreen in my car shattered and some splinters of glass apparently penetrated my corneas and spilt the vitreous humour—the transparent jelly inside the eyeballs.'

April was grateful that Hugh couldn't see the appalled look on her face. 'How are they going to fix that?' she asked.

He shrugged. 'Apparently the surgeon puts in a probe and sucks out the damaged jelly. Then down the same tube he trickles this solution of salt and chemicals that compensate for the lost jelly. And presto! Vision instantly restored.'

April felt squeamish just thinking about it. But she knew it was imperative she sounded confident about the success of the operation. 'Isn't it marvellous what they can do these days?' she enthused.

Hugh agreed, then quite unexpectedly took off his sunglasses and rubbed his eyes.

April could not help staring. After what Hugh had said she had been expecting some sort of damage, or scarring. But there was none. Not a scratch. His eyes were deep-set and quite beautiful. Not strictly blue. More a grey with a dark blue rim. But there were some lines around them and he did look older with his glasses off.

'Shouldn't you be leaving those on?' Harry growled. 'You know what the doctor said. Any glare is bad for you.'

Hugh grumbled. But he replaced the glasses.

April slid off the stool she was sitting on. 'I must go,' she said. 'I have plans to read at least four novels while I'm here, not to mention the acquiring of a tan. Thanks for the tea, Harry. And the loan of your towel, Hugh.' She slipped it from her shoulders and placed it on the counter.

'How about reading to me some time, April?' Hugh asked as she turned to leave.

She stood still. 'Oh...of course...if you like. What?'

'Anything you've got would do.'

She thought of the novels she had brought with her. All sexy, pacy best-sellers, not the sort of thing she would want to read aloud to Hugh. 'I'll see what Uncle Guy has in his bookshelves.'

'Fine. When?'

April bit her bottom lip. How could she refuse? 'I could come back some time after three. I don't like being out in the sun in the heat of the day. We could lie on the sand and I'll read to you.'

'Fine! She's a great girl, isn't she, Harry?'

Harry grunted again. It was amazing the range of Harry's grunts. This one was definitely a 'we'll just wait and see' grunt.

'I'll walk back with you,' Hugh offered, getting to his feet.

Fluster claimed April. 'Oh...you don't have to.'

'I know.'

It was clear he was determined to come with her for he was off the stool and out of the door in an instant. April breathed deeply in and out before following. As long as he didn't want to hold her hand again, she thought anxiously.

Hugh began speaking as soon as they were alone walking across the sand. 'I wanted to explain about Harry,' he started. 'I know he seems rude but there are reasons for his behaviour, April, reasons I'd like you to know.'

She couldn't find it in her heart to tell him she would rather not know, that all of a sudden she wanted to run away from Hugh and everything associated with him as fast as her legs could carry her.

But as her gaze slid hungrily over him, and her heart contracted, April knew that she would stay. She would stay and listen, she would stay and read to him, stay and let nature take its cruel, inevitable course.

CHAPTER FOUR

HUGH'S story about Harry proved very touching.

The poor man had had a dreadful childhood. Drunken, abusive parents. Repeated beatings. Interrupted schooling. No love and little chance at life.

At fourteen Harry had run away from home, and, being a big lad, was able to get a job as a builder's labourer. When he was old enough to secure a driver's licence he'd taken to driving interstate trucks. By the time he was twenty-five he had saved enough to buy his own truck. This in itself had been rewarding, but his need to have a family of his own was great.

He'd married a pretty blonde waitress and begun working doubly hard to provide a nice home for his wife and future children. He hadn't minded the long hours he'd had to put in, because he had a goal—a purpose in life.

But his new wife had not been so patient to get the good things in life. She'd introduced her husband to a friend of hers who had ideas on how to get rich quickly. Harry had reluctantly agreed to take part in a robbery at an empty millionaire's mansion, only to be caught. No sooner was he gaoled than his wife had begun divorce proceedings. Desperate, he'd attempted a foolhardy and disastrous escape. This had only increased his sentence and did nothing to stop the inevitable divorce.

Hugh had met Harry ten years later when he was asked by a Salvation Army chaplain to conduct art classes at the prison. Harry had surprised the warders by signing up for the sculpture section. Yet for six months all he had done during class, Hugh told April, was sit down at the back of the room, his arms folded, never saying a word. Then one day he'd come up to Hugh and said, 'I'd like to make something . . . in that stuff,' pointing to a piece of marble Hugh had brought in.

It had taken him ages but the simple form of a dog Harry fashioned was the best piece any student of Hugh's had ever produced. Their friendship had blossomed alongside their working relationship and Hugh's promise of a job and a room had helped obtain his early release.

Hugh's car accident had happened a couple of days before Harry got out of prison. He'd come to the hospital straight from the gaol, refusing to leave Hugh's bedside. When Hugh had needed someone to look after him in the long months of recuperation, Harry was the natural choice.

'I pay him of course,' Hugh remarked. 'Though I'm sure he'd do it for nothing.'

April agreed. There was more than a touch of hero-worship in Harry's feelings for Hugh. And she could understand that. Hugh was probably the first person to ever extend him a genuinely kind hand.

'I get the feeling, April,' he went on quietly, 'that, underneath his grunts, he quite likes you.'

April had to laugh at that. 'I don't think so.'

'I beg to differ. When he doesn't like someone he's very vocal. The things he said about Cynthia would make your toes curl.'

April's heart flipped over. 'Cynthia?'

'My fiancée,' Hugh announced, then laughed. It was not a happy sound. 'Wrong word...my *ex*-fiancée.'

They had come to the base of April's steps. When Hugh's hand reached out to hold the railing, she noticed his fist was clenched tightly around the wood, his knuckles white. 'There's no reason why you shouldn't know. Cynthia was driving when the accident occurred, ran into a car at an intersection. She wasn't hurt, except for a few minor bruises. It appears she was at my bedside for a couple of days. I was in a semi-coma so I don't remember. When the doctors told her I was blind she apparently took off the ring and left. I haven't seen her since.'

He let go of the railing and dragged in a deep breath, expanding his already broad chest. 'I think my experience has reinforced Harry's wary attitude to females. I'm sure that given a few days you and he will get along famously. He likes genuine people. And I feel that, despite your youthful impetuosity, you *are* genuine, April Jamieson. Very genuine indeed.'

His right hand found and tipped up her chin. Then he bent to brush her forehead with a light, very platonic kiss. 'Thank you,' he said warmly. 'For bringing me out of my shell, for offering your friendship when I needed it.'

April tried to speak, but couldn't. The lump in her throat was in danger of melting into tears.

'April?' He was frowning down at her. His hand had slipped down her slender neck to rest on her shoulder. 'Is there something wrong?'

She cleared her throat. 'No. Should there be?' Even to her ears she sounded strangled.

His frown remained. 'I guess not.'

'Well, then. I'll see you on the beach around three. OK?'

She turned from him without waiting for an answer and hurried up the steps.

April set off back down the beach shortly before three. Hugh was already sitting on the distant sand and as she approached she could see he was busily applying a sunscreen, first one arm and then the other.

She had the crazy urge to creep up on him and place her hands over his sunglasses while saying 'guess who?', knowing that it would make him laugh. But she didn't dare, fearing it might backfire on her if she touched him. Better to keep her hands right off!

How different the situation had been on this very beach last summer, with Max. He had been all hands, inviting her touch, seducing her with his sophisticated charm, making his intentions very clear.

April had been secretly infatuated with Max for some time—one of the reasons she had accompanied her uncle to exhibitions at his gallery so often. But Max had never noticed her till suddenly he had found himself alone at his beach-house last summer after his latest dolly-bird had left in a huff. April had been staying at the cove with Uncle Guy, whose idea of a holiday was to read and sleep a lot, leaving her to her own devices.

Stupid, naïve April had not realised till long afterwards that it had hardly been honourable of Max to try to seduce the young niece of a friend. But she now appreciated what a lucky escape she'd had from his lecherous clutches.

April's gaze raked over Hugh's beautiful, semi-naked body as she dropped on the sand beside him. Instinct told her that Hugh would not scoff at her virginity as Max had done. It made her unhappy that he thought her loose in that regard.

'Aaah.' A wide smile split his face as he turned towards her. 'Florence Nightingale has returned. Now what splendid tome have you brought to read to me? Harold Robbins? Jackie Collins?' His insinuation was clear. A modern young girl like herself would only read books whose characters reflected *modern* values.

April was hurt. Then defiant. He had no right to judge her so harshly. Nor did he have to keep on mocking and teasing her. If he kept it up, she vowed, he might find a hard-cover edition of *Hollywood Husbands* stuffed between his perfect teeth!

'Sorry,' she said sweetly. 'I've already read all the Harold Robbinses and Jackie Collinses at least three times. I've even marked the juicy bits for repeated perusals.'

'*Touché,*' Hugh muttered. 'All right, what *have* you brought?'

'*High Stakes.*'

'*High Stakes*? Who wrote that?'

'Dick Francis.'

'I haven't read any of his.'

'Neither have I.' He was a favourite author of her uncle, so April figured a man should like the stories.

Hugh squeezed some lotion down his legs and began massaging it in. April looked away. 'Shall I begin?' she suggested briskly.

'In a sec.' Now he was smoothing the cream over his shoulders. 'Got your sunscreen on?'

'Yes.' She always applied hers while naked if she planned wearing a bikini. And there seemed no point in not wearing hers now.

April glanced down at the skimpy red garment with a certain irony. At least Harry couldn't accuse her of dressing to seduce a blind man. But she had quite deliberately not put on any perfume. Somehow she sensed that old eagle-eye would notice the slightest suggestive move she made towards Hugh, which seemed ridiculous considering Hugh's attitude to her.

Yet despite her irritation April was moved by the big man's protective devotion. It bespoke a caring nature beneath his tough, gruff exterior.

'Here!' Hugh extended his hand with the tube resting in his palm. 'Put some on my back, will you? I can't reach properly.'

She stared aghast at the outstretched object for a moment before taking it. 'And what did you do before I came along?' she almost snapped.

'Contortions.'

'Really!' She squeezed a large dob into her palm and slapped it on his back.

'Hey! That's cold,' he protested. 'You could have warmed it up in your palm for a while.'

'Oh, for goodness' sake! What a baby!' She did, however, stop lathering it on quite so ruthlessly, slowing her hand movement to a more reasonable speed.

But with the slowing came the dreaded heightened awareness. His skin was so smooth. And hairless. Like satin. Cool, silky, sensuous satin...

April found herself swallowing hard, trying not to let her fingers linger on his rippling muscles longer than necessary. 'I think I've put too much cream on,' she said in a choked voice. 'It won't sink in.'

'Just keep doing what you're doing,' Hugh sighed. 'It feels marvellous.'

Against all the dictates of her conscience and common sense, she knelt up closer behind him, kneading and caressing, smoothing and soothing till the nerves in her stomach had turned into other more disturbing sensations.

There was no fooling herself. She was becoming sexually aroused. Totally. Thoroughly.

She had known she would if she touched him. Known it from her first sight of his naked beauty. And as she continued to touch him, her throat grew drier. Her body ached. Her fingers trembled.

'You're ripe and ready for a lover, April,' Max had told her after she'd confessed her lack of experience. 'Just be grateful I didn't take advantage of the fact...'

She hadn't been grateful at the time.

'I could take this treatment forever,' Hugh murmured dreamily, stretching back into her hands.

The sudden contact of his shoulder-blades with the hardened points of her breasts shocked April. She pushed him upright. 'That's enough. I came here to read to you, not be your personal slave!'

Oh, God, she groaned silently, let me be your personal slave. Let me...

'Very well, o, callous one.' Hugh rolled over and stretched out on his front. 'Read away. But don't blame me if I go to sleep. I feel so relaxed now.'

He might feel relaxed. *Her* nerves were at screaming-point!

April took her time, finding a comfortable position in the sand before opening the paperback at the first page. Taking a deep breath, she began to read. Typical, she thought grimly, a few pages later. A novel about rejection.

'Surely that's not all?' Hugh joked when she hesitated.

'Oh, shut up, or you can get Harry to read to you.'

'Impossible.'

'Nothing's impossible.'

'Harry can't read.'

April's heart sagged. Once again she felt guilty, once again she had allowed herself to become consumed with her own feelings when the people around her had major, heart-wrenching problems in life to deal with. A broken engagement, blindness, illiteracy.

She felt terrible. 'Oh, Hugh... The poor man...'

'Yes,' he agreed. 'I was going to teach him before this damned accident happened. He wouldn't go to night-school. He said he couldn't bear to be laughed at.'

'Don't tell me any more or I'll cry.'

He leant over and patted her arm. 'You really are a softie, aren't you? Better toughen up, love, or the world will eat you for breakfast. At least...that's what Harry's advice always is.'

'And what's your advice?' she asked, her voice catching.

'I wouldn't be looking to *me* for any advice on life's problems just now if I were you,' he said with a wealth of self-mockery. 'Though funnily enough I used to think I had all the answers, that I knew exactly where I was going and what I wanted from life. I watched the poor decisions others made with their choices in careers and life partners, and I was sure I had successfully avoided all the pitfalls. There I was, making a name in the art world and about to enter into what I thought was the perfect marriage, when whammo! Everything went black—in more ways than one! Believe me, April, going blind certainly gives you a new perspective.' He laughed at his own sick joke. 'Though at least you find out who your real friends are!'

'Don't you have any family, Hugh?' she asked, upset by the lonely bitter sound in his voice.

'No. My parents were middle-aged when they had me. They've been dead a few years now. I have a couple of distant cousins scattered around Australia. But no one close.'

'How did you start sculpting?' she went on, hoping to get his mind off his accident, and its subsequent unhappiness.

'Both Mum and Dad were artists. Dad, a painter. Mum, a potter. One of their friends was a sculptor—and a fascinating man. When I was thirteen I used to go over to his studio, pretending I wanted to learn his craft, just to hear the stories he told. But before I knew it I was hooked.'

'He sounds an interesting man.'

'He was. But he's dead now. Cirrhosis of the liver, the death certificate said. A broken heart, more accurately,' he finished sharply.

'What happened?'

'He fell in love with one of his students—a girl over twenty years younger than himself. Married her after a whirlwind courtship.'

'And?'

'The inevitable happened, of course. After six months the honeymoon was well and truly over. At least for her! She simply upped one day, said he bored her to death, and left, moved in with another of his students, a twenty-year-old. Garrick was simply devastated. He started drinking and didn't stop till he was six feet under. Such a rotten waste, and all because he let his heart rule his head! He was crazy to marry such a young girl. Simply crazy!'

April blinked at Hugh's virulence, understanding dawning at why he was so scornful of the young. And students in particular. Obviously his mentor's decline and death had made a lasting impression on his teenage mind, making him think all young people were not to be trusted in matters of faithfulness. His being an only child to elderly parents would also have contributed to what she thought was an overly serious turn of mind.

But what good was this new understanding of Hugh's attitude? If anything, it underlined the futility of feeling anything for him other than friendship. She dragged in a deep breath, letting it out with a weary sigh.

'Something tells me,' Hugh said drily, 'that Dick Francis is not going to get a good hearing today. What say we have a siesta instead?'

April pulled herself together, determined to concentrate on being the friend he needed. 'Definitely not!' she declared. 'We're going to reach page one hundred by five o'clock. Then tomorrow we'll finish it. Now... I'll begin again...'

CHAPTER FIVE

APRIL was wrong.

They finished the book that day, both becoming so engrossed that they couldn't put it down. Even when Harry insisted they come up to eat, the book went with them, April reading while they devoured hamburgers and beer.

Harry said they were 'bonkers' to let a book get them in like that, and left to do some night rock-fishing.

April finished the last line with a satisfied sigh shortly after nine. 'Our hero showed those baddies a thing or two, didn't he?' she said, glancing over at Hugh who was stretched out in an armchair, ankles and arms crossed. It looked as if his eyes were closed beneath the sunglasses. 'You haven't gone to sleep, have you?'

'Nope,' came the curt answer. 'Just thinking.'

'About the book?'

'About the book. And life...'

Her chest tightened, knowing instinctively that Hugh was thinking about his fiancée, about how she had left him when he needed her most.

April's heart turned over. What hell he must have gone through! To wake up in hospital, broken and blind, desperately needing the comfort that could only come from family and loved ones. But there'd been no family to hold his hand. And no loved one...

'What about life?' she asked softly, half hoping that he would confide in her.

He sat up straight, tension in every line of his body. 'A young girl like you doesn't want to have serious discussions about life.'

'Will you stop saying things like that?' she snapped. 'I've told you before. I'm almost twenty-one. A lot of women my age are already married and having babies.'

'Unfortunately true,' he scoffed. 'And in a few years they'll be divorced, with problem children on their hands.'

April could only shake her head at Hugh's continuing outbursts of cynicism. She understood that he had reason to be bitter over what Cynthia had done. And she accepted it wasn't easy for him during these countdown days to his operation. But it wasn't doing him any favours if she let him use her as some sort of whipping-boy.

'You really have to stop lumping people together into boxes, Hugh,' she debated firmly. 'Not all young people are flighty. Or unfaithful. I don't know what gets into you sometimes, picking on my age as if it's a dirty word. I suppose your Cynthia was young, was she? Like that girl your teacher fell in love with?'

His laugh was very, very dry. 'Cynthia happens to be thirty-two. And, before you add two and two together and make five again, she's also intelligent and cool and calm and independently wealthy. As I said before, she was perfect...'

April was stunned. And even more confused. Why, then, had Cynthia left? Was it just an inability to accept a husband who was handicapped, even temporarily? What kind of love was *that* if it disappeared so readily? April accepted it wouldn't be easy to deal with blindness—one could see how difficult it had made Hugh—but she felt instinctively she couldn't have left her fiancé if she had been in Cynthia's place, even if he'd been permanently blind.

'She couldn't have loved you very deeply, Hugh, if she left you like that,' April voiced aloud. 'You're better off without her. Some women——'

'For God's sake, leave it alone, will you?' Hugh bit out, leaping to his feet. He went to move forward and immediately banged his shin on the edge of the coffee-table. He swore volubly and bent down to rub his leg.

April's first instinct was to race over and help him. But some inner voice warned her not to do so.

'I don't know how you can stand yourself, Hugh Davies,' she reproached. 'You're not the first person who's been dumped in this world. You should be grateful that you're not going to be permanently blind as well. If it weren't for my feeling sorry for Harry having to put up with you, I'd walk out of here right now and never speak to you again, let alone read you any more books!'

There were a few moments of charged silence. Then suddenly, Hugh tipped back his head and laughed. 'My God, but you're precious! I honestly don't know what I would have done if you hadn't come along.'

'You'd have kept breathing and hopefully stopped feeling sorry for yourself!'

He chuckled again. 'What did you say you were going to be? An economist? I would have thought the army would have suited you better. Stand up straight there, Hugh Davies. Chin up, stomach in, eyes straight forward.' He did just that, holding his body to attention. 'How's that, Sarge?'

April swung her eyes away from his taut muscles. 'Just passable, for such an old, *old* soldier.'

'Ouch.'

Just then, Harry made an appearance on the balcony outside, a couple of fish on his line. 'Harry's back,' April informed Hugh. 'I'd best be going.'

'Do you have to? I was just beginning to enjoy myself.'

'Is that so? You mean you didn't enjoy all those hours I was reading to you? That's gratitude for you!'

'Why don't you stay for supper?' he urged.

She ignored the desire to do just that, fearing how this man made her feel by just being in the same room as he. 'I don't think so, Hugh. I'm rather tired. I'll see you tomorrow afternoon. About three again? On the beach?'

'You'll bring another Dick Francis with you?'

'I'll certainly bring something.' Much safer all round to have something concrete to do, she thought ruefully. 'Bye.' She walked over and kissed him on the cheek, thinking to herself that it was the bravest, most stupid thing she could do. 'Good-night. Sleep tight.'

'You too.'

But of course she didn't sleep tight. She didn't sleep till sheer exhaustion won the day near dawn.

'I thought you weren't coming!' Hugh accused when she finally made an appearance down his end of the beach around four the next afternoon. 'Did you bring another book with you?'

'No.'

'Why not?'

'Absence makes the heart grow fonder,' she tossed off, thinking ruefully that never a truer word had been spoken. In the hours she had been away from Hugh she hadn't stopped thinking about him. 'Dick Francis will appear on every second day,' she added firmly.

He groaned. 'You would have made a splendid SS Kommandant, April Jamieson.'

'Good! Then obey orders. Today we are going to do a cryptic crossword.' She had come fully armed, with an old newspaper. Not to mention a dictionary, two biros, and a beach umbrella. It was far too hot to sit in the sun indefinitely, she decided. Neither was she going to torture herself every day putting on Hugh's sunscreen.

With businesslike efficiency she arranged every-thing, making Hugh sit in the shade. 'Now,' she began firmly. 'One across: stolen near the equator...three letters...'

* * *

It turned out to be a surprisingly enjoyable two weeks, with both April and Harry conspiring together to take Hugh's mind off his coming trauma. Between the Dick Francis books and the crosswords, they swam, sunbathed and fished. Harry cooked them all sorts of interesting foods, once again surprising April. She discovered that, though illiterate, he was a man of many talents, with a huge capacity for kindness and caring. Soon, they were firm friends.

Her feelings for Hugh were still not clear-cut in her mind. Oh, they were firm friends too. There was no doubt about that. Hugh obviously liked having her around, even though he continued to tease and patronise her in the most irritating fashion.

She gave as good as she got, but she was finding it harder and harder to control the sexual side of her feelings. On the whole she had successfully buried her urges—except in her dreams—but occasionally her body betrayed her, and she would find herself staring at him with a very real and fierce hunger. Mostly she hid it, even from Harry's sharp eyes. But she was grateful that Harry was not present during the incident that occurred on the last afternoon of their stay at the cove.

Harry had driven into town to buy some Chinese food for their final meal together and, since it was stiflingly hot, April and Hugh went swimming. When they emerged from the sea at around four o'clock, it was still too hot to lie in the sun, so the two of them made for the cool of inside.

Hugh went confidently ahead, forgetting perhaps that the soles of his feet were still wet and that the stone steps could become slippery. April was right behind him when, half a dozen steps up, he lost his footing. Arms and legs flailing, he crashed back on to her so that they both went tumbling backwards.

Whether by design or accident Hugh was able to grab April's arms then spin her round so that he, not herself, took the brunt of the fall, his back hitting the sand first with her body being cushioned by his. She landed sprawled half sideways across him, her breasts pressing into his stomach, her lips brushing a male nipple, one of her hands up around his neck, the other wedged firmly between his thighs.

For a second they lay winded, with April not daring to move that hand from its embarrassing position.

'Are you all right?' Hugh asked.

'Y-yes ... Are you?' Her voice held a breathless, husky quality.

'Fine ... I think ...'

Her cheeks flamed as she lifted her head to stare down at the precariously placed hand. Its side was pressed against his swimming-costume and as she shakily withdrew it she could do nothing to prevent her index finger and thumb grazing across the damp material in an intimate retreat.

The gasp was Hugh's, not hers.

'Hell,' he muttered, his body leaping into arousal with startling speed.

Mortified, April scrambled to her feet, not knowing where to look or what to do. Her heart was thudding painfully in her chest, her throat dry. Best to ignore it, she thought frantically. Pretend she hadn't noticed.

'Here...take my hand,' she offered hurriedly.

His grip closed warm and firm around hers, but when he hesitated she said, 'Are you sure you're all right?'

He made a sound deep in his throat that could have been impatience, or frustration. 'No permanent damage,' he growled, then put his weight against the pull of her hand. April was relieved to see that by the time he rose his body was almost back to normal.

'Perhaps I'd better help you up the steps,' she suggested, not really wanting to but knowing she should. Her heart was still pounding from the incident, her palms uncomfortably clammy.

His refusal was swift and sharp. 'No, thanks. I can manage.'

He was angry. Angry, and embarrassed.

Another time, with another woman—Cynthia perhaps—his arousal might be a wished-for occurrence. With her, it had been an annoyance.

The thought depressed April. Unbearably. But, as she lifted unhappy eyes to his grim face, another more devastating realisation hit. She loved Hugh, loved him with all the boundless love her young heart was ready to give. There was no denying it. It surrounded and consumed her, making everything she had ever felt for anyone else seem shallow and worthless.

It was a realisation that brought real pain, a pain that contracted her heart, twisted her stomach, made her want to cry. How could she have let it happen? He would never love her back. Never! Not only that, it was the last thing she wanted for herself this year, the very last thing...

April's gaze travelled over him as he turned to place a careful foot on the first step, the knowledge of her love making her want to touch him more than ever. How wonderful it must be to make love with someone you loved, she thought yearningly. To be able to kiss them, hold them, caress them, join with them...

April was thankful now that she had not thrown her virginity away on someone like Max. But what dismayed her unbearably was that she would never get an opportunity to give herself to the man she loved, this man who even now was walking away from her, who tomorrow would go back to Sydney, and a life that was unlikely to have a place for her, even as a friend.

'Hugh!' she called out as he reached the balcony.

He stopped, and turned slowly.

'I don't think I'll come up just now. I'd like to shampoo my hair before tonight. Harry wants me over here by seven at the latest,' he said. 'You didn't need me for anything, did you?'

He said nothing for a couple of seconds, setting her nerves on edge. She hoped and prayed he didn't need help with anything.

'No... You go on. I'll see you later.'

Relieved but still miserable, she turned away and hurried across the hot sand.

CHAPTER SIX

IT WAS terribly hot.

April stood naked in the bedroom and tried to decide what to wear. Finally she dragged on a pair of white shorts and a red T-shirt, hating the touch of any clothing at all on her sticky skin.

She didn't bother with a hair-drier, letting her freshly shampooed curls lie in damp relief around her neck. She had no intention of bothering with make-up either, since Hugh couldn't see, and Harry wouldn't give a hoot.

But when the thought crossed her mind that one day soon Hugh would no longer be blind, she walked over to stare in the dressing-table mirror, wondering if it would make any difference when and if he saw her.

She had attractive hair. Everyone said so. Thick and black, layered to take advantage of its natural curl, it framed her oval face, touching her shoulders, dipping slightly down at the back. Her eyes were her next best feature, being dark blue and widely set, with long black lashes.

She frowned at her mouth, never having felt happy with it since the headmistress at school had called it pouty.

And then of course there was her figure. What a shame she was so short. April had always thought that more height was needed to carry her overgenerous curves. She didn't regret her full bust, but there was much too much bottom, she considered with a grimace.

A sudden wave of depression took hold of her, making her sink down dejectedly on to the water-bed. She knew in her heart that her looks would not sway Hugh. He had spelt everything out very clearly. She was too young for him. Besides, she had the awful feeling he wasn't over the break-up with Cynthia yet.

April sighed and stood up, absently picking up a bottle of perfume that was lying on the dressing-table and spraying herself with it. It was called Destiny, an exotic musky fragrance, obviously left behind by one of her uncle's lady-loves.

Hugh and Harry were lounging in deck-chairs, drinking beer, when she arrived. Harry got up immediately, telling her to take his chair while he got her a glass of the white wine she preferred.

'Thanks,' she murmured as she settled next to Hugh. He was wearing bright Bermuda shorts and nothing else, a fact that had April staring resolutely out to sea.

'You're wearing perfume,' he remarked in an abrupt tone. 'You don't usually wear perfume.'

She found his brusqueness upsetting. Most men complimented a woman's perfume, not castigated it. 'I'm sorry you don't like it,' she said irritably. 'Shall I move further away?'

'That might be a bloody good idea!'

She stared at him. 'What's got into you tonight?'

'It's this heat,' he growled, and downed the rest of the beer. 'Would you believe Harry wants to play poker after dinner? I told him it was impossible but he said you and I could collaborate. You're supposed to sit next to me and tell me what cards I'm holding.'

The idea of sitting close to Hugh all night brought a squirming sensation to her stomach. 'I'm not sure that would work,' came the hesitant comment. She looked across to see Hugh's forehead wrinkling in a dark frown, so she added with a quick laugh, 'I'm a good poker player myself and we might argue over what cards to throw in.'

A short, impatient sound rumbled in his throat.

Harry reappeared with her drink. He handed it over before disappearing again. April glanced across at Hugh, her gaze unconsciously drifting down to his powerfully muscled thighs. The memory of what had happened that afternoon brought a tide of heat to her cheeks.

'What are you thinking?'

April jumped at the sudden question. 'Oh ... I—er——'

'Come on. Be honest.'

Her laugh was self-mocking. 'I don't think you'd really want to know.' She took a large gulp of the wine.

'I'm game.'

'Are you?' She couldn't help the heavy irony in her voice. Hugh picked up on it immediately, for his head jerked round to glare at her. With the sun having set he had taken his glasses off, and the impact of his sightless yet intense gaze was unnerving.

'You really think I'm an old stick-in-the-mud, don't you, April?'

She was in no mood to humour him. 'If the cap fits...'

A flash of fury swept over his features. 'That's so easily said, isn't it? Would you prefer I do as this modern generation does? Give in to every whim I get, every urge I feel?'

She was shocked by his unexpected anger.

'Do you know how I feel tonight?' he went on quite savagely. 'Tomorrow we head back to Sydney, and in two days I'll be in that bloody hospital, having that bloody operation. I hate the uncertainty, the doubts. Hate the way it all makes me feel. Weak, helpless!'

'Oh, Hugh, you shouldn't...'

'Shouldn't what?' he snapped. 'Shouldn't swear? Shouldn't worry? God, April, I'm going *mad* with worry, not to mention...' He broke off and ran a shaking hand through his hair. 'I crave... distraction. What do you suggest I do? Race you off for a quickie?' He was gripping his beer glass with finger-bruising strength. 'If you're as sexy as you smell, I'd surely sleep afterwards!'

Harry popped his head outside. 'Chow's on,' he informed brightly. 'Come on, Hugh, April.'

April scrambled to her feet immediately and went inside, her face white, her insides trembling.

The tension at the beginning of the meal was palpable and in the course of things April drank more wine than she should have. Hugh was not slow on imbibing either and by the time they had finished their banquet of several dishes he was even more caustic and cynical than usual.

Harry gave April a frowning glance, and suggested they begin the poker as soon as he had disposed of the dirty dishes. They did so, but it was as bad as April feared, sitting so close to Hugh. Their bare thighs were pressed together along one side, and she had to whisper in his ear to prevent Harry from knowing what cards they held.

The third deal of cards saw Hugh and April disagreeing, ostensibly over what cards to discard. April had her way, keeping a pair of kings instead of going for a flush. Unfortunately the first card she drew was a club, the very suit she would have needed if Hugh's will had prevailed. There were no further kings, however.

'See what I get for listening to a female?' Hugh scoffed. 'I think I should take her over my knee and paddle her backside.'

Harry's shaggy eyebrows shot skywards. 'I think you've had too much to drink, mate.'

'Who, me? My partner here's the one who's sloshed.'

April sighed and stood up, her whole body tense with suppressed emotion. 'I think we'd better give the cards a miss, don't you? How about I make us some coffee?'

Harry yawned. 'None for me, thanks. I think I'll hit the sack. Wine does strange things to me.' Which was patently clear when he nearly walked into his bedroom door as he left the room.

'Well, Hugh?' she said tightly. 'Coffee for you?'

His negative grunt was the last straw.

'In that case I don't want any either,' she snapped. 'I'm going for a swim then I'm off home. It's a long drive back tomorrow.'

His brooding silence had her shaking her head and leaving, her emotions only just in control. She marched down to the water, stripped off all her clothes and plunged defiantly naked into the sea, swimming out into the dark waters like a person possessed.

After a few minutes Hugh surprised her by making an appearance at the water's edge. 'You shouldn't be swimming on your own, April!' he shouted wearily. 'You might get a cramp. I could hardly save you. And Harry's out like a light.'

'Go to hell, Hugh!' she shouted back.

'Can't,' he growled. 'I'm already there.'

His obvious wretchedness totally defused her anger. What on earth are you doing, April? she asked herself. Hasn't the man got enough troubles? OK, so he drank too much and was beastly and rude. So what?

She sighed and began swimming back to shore. At least she was sober now. She hauled her naked form from the water and after a slight hesitation began walking towards him. The moonlight showed every inch of her nudity and she had to keep telling herself he couldn't really see. A nervous flutter rose and fell in her chest as she drew up to him, for he appeared to be looking right at her breasts.

'Aah, so there you are,' Hugh muttered, sensing her presence. 'Well? I suppose you're waiting for an apology.'

'Not really.'

'Then what are you waiting for?'

She swallowed. 'You're standing on my clothes.'

He froze for a moment, then bent down and picked them up.

April watched, shivering, as he felt each piece. Shorts, T-shirt, white lace bikini briefs. 'You don't wear much.' The words sounded thick.

She stepped forward and held out an unsteady hand. 'Would you give them to me, please?' Her damp skin was breaking out into goose-bumps. Her stomach was in knots. 'Please, Hugh...'

He just stood there, not making a move, not saying a word.

What devil was it in her that made her do what she did next? Who knew? All human beings were good and bad, light and dark. And love made one daring...

With tremulous fingers she took the clothes from his hands, then dropped them on the sand before bridging the final space between them. Hugh's gasp of shock sent a hot jab of arousal through her body.

'Hugh,' she whispered in a voice reserved for sirens. It was low and husky. Sweet and inviting.

Her arms slid up around his neck, the contact of her swollen nipples with his chest making her shiver. But not with cold now. She moved against him, sending more currents of electric pleasure all through her.

Hugh groaned, and for a brief ecstatic moment held her close. Then suddenly he was disengaging her arms, pulling back from her. 'No, April. No...'

'Why not?' This time she wrapped her arms around his waist and sank into his warmth. 'I want to touch you. Don't you want to touch me too?'

'Oh, God,' Hugh rasped. 'This is madness. *Madness*, I tell you!'

'Then let it be madness,' she urged, raining moist kisses on his chest. Her hands slid up over his back in a sensuous trail.

'You don't know what you're inviting!'

The blood was pounding in her veins and the words came—mindless and passionate. 'Yes, I do.'

The tip of her tongue grazed over his skin and he groaned again, a tortured despairing sound, but his hands were already reaching to hold and lift her face, his mouth searching for hers, finding it, forcing it open. His kiss probed and plundered without mercy, demanding an equally uninhibited response, sweeping aside all April's misconceptions that her first time would be a tender, sweet experience.

There was no persuasion or seduction in Hugh's actions. Somewhere in the back of her dazed mind, April knew that, while he was taking what she had so blatantly offered, his lovemaking had a harsh, angry quality to it, as though despite being devastatingly aroused he was hating himself for it.

His hands grazed down over her shoulders, down, down, till they were moulding her buttocks, cupping them so as to press her into him, then half lifting her till she fitted his body to perfection. Her thighs had parted and her hot aching flesh curved around his thinly clad loins. She was feverishly aware of his pulsating hardness, pushing, demanding, and the urge to blend her body with his was so strong that their union seemed inevitable.

'Yes, Hugh,' she panted, dragging her mouth away from him. 'Yes... Please, yes.'

His breathing was as heavy as her own. He let her go, her body sliding down his till trembling toes touched the wet sand. He pulled back a fraction, then slowly his hands began to roam over her body, tracing her curves, as though imprinting her shape on his mind.

She stood still, breathless with pleasure as his hands caressed her breasts, moaning with disappointment when they moved on. But she was not to be disappointed for long. His slender, knowing fingers had a more devastating goal, making her cry out when they slipped between her thighs. They found and explored her moist womanhood, stroking and caressing with considerable expertise till soft, panting sounds were coming from her throat. Her own hands had closed over his shoulders, their bruising grip echoing the growing tension inside her. When she suddenly dug her nails into his flesh, he dragged her hands away.

'Here... touch me,' he commanded, holding her palm against his own throbbing need.

Somehow they had moved into the shallows, but April was oblivious of the water lapping around their legs. She was without thought, her whole being concentrating on what lay beneath her hand. She thrilled to Hugh's moans when she caressed him, each muffled cry sending fierce flames of desire through every vein in her body. Before she knew it he had discarded his shorts and was guiding her hand back to hard, naked flesh.

But even as her fingers moved to touch him once more he pushed them aside, sweeping her up into his arms and carrying her to the shore, stretching her out and covering her. She, in turn, opened eagerly to his imminent possession, already moving her hips in a slow, sensuous rhythm.

It never crossed her mind that her body, her ignited excited body would feel any pain, and when it ripped through her like a knife slicing into her flesh she could not stifle the instinctive cry nor prevent the involuntary recoil.

'What the...?' Hugh froze, then abruptly withdrew.

April grabbed him by the shoulders. 'No, don't stop! Please, Hugh...'

But he abandoned her, cursing. 'Good God in heaven, girl!' His voice was shaking, as was his body. 'Why didn't you tell me?' He rolled away then sat up, his breathing heavy and laboured, his face in agony.

Her disappointment at his stopping was almost as acute as her distress at his anger. 'Hugh, please...'

His groan was tortured. 'That's all I need, you begging me to go on.'

A ghastly dismay was creeping into her heart. 'But Hugh, I...I wanted you to make love to me. I still do.' She reached out to touch his thigh but he angrily swept her hand aside.

'That much was obvious, girlie.'

'Don't call me that!' she cried. I'm a woman, she wanted to scream at him. A woman. And I love you...

'And why not? That's all you are! A girl, a silly young girl, and a virgin to boot. What in the hell did you think you were playing at here tonight? Good God!'

'But Hugh...' She was struggling for words. 'I'm almost twenty-one. I... I can't stay a virgin forever.'

'Well, I've got no intention of being the one to start you on your merry way!'

April's heart plummeted. What was the use? How could she say that she wanted him to be her first lover even if he didn't love her back; that it would have been a memory she would have treasured forever?

Shattered, miserable, she dragged herself up into a sitting position. Her muscles were beginning to stiffen and there was a dull throbbing in her temples. 'Well, you didn't, did you?' she murmured, pressing her hands against the sides of her face. 'You stopped,' she repeated dully.

'And thank God I did! What if you'd got pregnant? Did you think of that? No, of course not. As I've said before, just a silly little fool looking for kicks without considering the consequences.'

'I'm on the Pill,' she said in a weary, wretched fashion. She had continued taking it even after she had seen the light about Max, for the simple reason that it alleviated her extremely painful periods.

'I might have known!' He shook his head in total exasperation. 'What gets into girls like you? Do you all go on the Pill as a matter of course, just in case you get the urge one night? Then what, April? Another lover, then another and another, till you can't remember their names or what they did to you?'

'Who are you to pass judgement, Hugh Davies?' she shot back at him. 'You would have taken me, if I hadn't been a virgin. Stop being holier than thou.'

'Much to my discredit, I assure you,' he returned bitterly. 'My only excuse is that I've been drinking. And it's been a long time since I had sex.'

A shudder went through April. The heat of passion was gone, cooled by cold, hard reality. Hugh had not desired her, April Jamieson. Frustration and alcohol had made him vulnerable to her provocative advances.

'I suppose I should apologise,' he muttered. 'Though damn it all, April, you were asking for it.'

'I don't usually act that way,' she said in desperate defence. 'I had too much to drink, too.'

'Well, keep off it in future! Exercise a little control.'

His preachy attitude was beginning to infuriate her. 'Oh, don't be ridiculous! I've had a few drinks before and not tried seducing the first male in sight. But it's inevitable that one day I would want to sleep with a man,' she tossed off, ready to say anything except that she loved him. 'I'm at that age.'

'And what stupid age would that be?' he growled.

'You know very well. The age of sexual experimentation. It happens to everyone, sooner or later,' she continued. 'There comes a time when you just have to know what it's like. I went on the Pill as a sensible precaution, not as a free ticket to promiscuity.'

'But that's what it will become, April, don't you see?'

'Look, Hugh, you're my friend, not my keeper. I don't have to answer to you, OK? Let's just forget any of this happened. I'm freezing and tired and I'd like to go to bed.' She scrambled to her feet and began dragging on her clothes.

It was only when she was fully dressed that she remembered Hugh's shorts. Oh, dear, she thought wearily, spotting them lying in a soggy heap at the water's edge. She supposed she'd have to go and get them. She couldn't get out of helping him back up to the beach-house but there was no way she was going to do that while he was still nude.

'Your shorts,' she said, red-faced, as she handed them over. 'They're wet, I'm afraid.'

'No hassle.'

She looked away while he put them on. 'Here's my hand,' she offered once he was dressed. They walked in silence and, despite holding hands, Hugh kept his distance and did not ask for extra support up the steps.

'April...' He turned to her once they reached the landing. 'I've been thinking... When we get back to Sydney... I'll understand if you don't want to see me again. Please don't feel you *have* to visit me in the hospital.'

Her heart took a nose-dive. She'd already accepted that their friendship might eventually dwindle away, but she hadn't been prepared for such a swift severance. She couldn't let him go. Not just yet...

'But why, Hugh?' she asked in the calmest voice she could muster. 'Surely not because of tonight?'

'Yes...because of tonight.'

Her laugh portrayed a light attitude. 'Don't be silly, Hugh. We both had too much to drink, as you said, and got carried away, that's all. I don't blame you one bit.'

His face was grim as he turned and moved slowly away from her, his hand reaching out till it found the railing. 'Well, I do. I shouldn't have let it go that far. I almost used you as nothing more than a sex object.'

'But you didn't, Hugh,' she argued. 'You wouldn't do a thing like that.'

He gave a short, sharp laugh. 'Don't go giving me too many virtues. You're not in my body just now.'

She blushed and the silence between them lengthened.

'I suppose I am being a touch melodramatic,' he said at last.

'You certainly are. Besides,' she went on, adopting a lighter note, 'you don't have that many friends that you can afford to throw away one as tolerant as me! Look what I've put up with these last two weeks. Nothing but patronising put-me-downs and never-ending teasings. ''Oh, but April, what would you know, you're so *young*!''' she mimicked.

He grimaced. 'Bad as that, eh? Well, you certainly didn't *feel* young tonight, my friend,' he admitted. 'That's the problem.'

More heat zoomed into her cheeks but she said nothing.

'I don't want to hurt you, April.'

'You...you wouldn't hurt me, Hugh,' she rasped.

'I might if I made love to you without loving you.'

'I see,' she choked out. 'And what if I said I wanted you to make love to me, whether you loved me or not?'

He sucked in a startled breath.

'Just testing,' she joked. It was amazing how carefree one could sound, even when one's heart was crumbling into pieces. 'See you in the morning.' Then without waiting for a reply she said goodnight and moved swiftly down the steps, her feet breaking into a run as soon as they reached the sand. She ran and ran, tears blinding her way, but even as she ran, faster and faster, she knew that was no escape from the hopeless love that burned in her heart.

CHAPTER SEVEN

THE drive back to Sydney the next day was long and hot. April had a difficult task keeping her mind on the road, which wasn't wise since it was Sunday, and the weekend flow of traffic was heavy.

She hadn't seen Hugh alone that morning, having stopped by the beach-house only long enough to say goodbye and to promise to come and see him in hospital on the Tuesday evening. He was to be operated on that morning, and, from what she'd been told, should be fit for visitors by then.

She might have been imagining it but she thought he'd been rather stiff in his manner towards her, Harry being the one to make most of the conversation. Perhaps he'd felt embarrassed by what had happened the night before. Guilty, even. April had made an extra effort to act her normal breezy self, but it hadn't been easy, and she was almost glad to get away.

By the time she pulled up outside her uncle's terrace-house in Balmain several hours later she had resigned herself to her so-called friendship with Hugh fading away once he got his sight back. He would plunge back into his work and totally forget about her, his need for the distraction of her company no longer there.

Feeling depressed, she was relieved when she let herself inside to find that her uncle was not at home.

He had left a note for her on the kitchen table, saying he was attending a society afternoon tea. There was a postscript announcing that last week he had secured a contract to write a gossipy by-line in one of the dailies.

A small smile came to her lips as she put the note back down on the table and began making herself a cup of tea. She could just see him now, dressed in his best Pierre Cardin suit, eating cucumber sandwiches and charming all the ladies, while extracting the most intimate and personal details with the ease of a magician pulling a rabbit out of a hat.

Her uncle loved gossip, loved to hear the latest scandal, and people seemed to like confiding in him. Perhaps it was because he was such a good listener, and never acted shocked by whatever people did.

April frowned. Would he be shocked if she told him what had happened up at the cove between herself and Hugh? How would he have reacted, she wondered, if Hugh had reciprocated her feelings and they had by now become lovers?

The answer came back immediately. He would definitely not approve of her becoming involved with a man of Hugh's age and experience.

April's sigh was agitated. Perhaps her uncle would be quite right. As Hugh had been right. Perhaps she *was* too young for him. She had to forget that he didn't look his age. The fact remained that he *was* thirty-four, a serious-thinking man with a conservative outlook—not a dolly-chasing trendsetter like Max. Hugh clearly found a twenty-year-old girl juvenile and childish by comparison to the sort of women he was used to going out with. The dreaded Cynthia had been thirty-two. Unlike Max, Hugh obviously didn't want to indulge in one casual affair after another. He wanted a lasting re- lationship, with a mature woman, as evidenced by his engagement the year before.

Tears pricked at April's eyes and her chin began to quiver. It was all very well to work things through sensibly. What had sense ever had to do with matters of the heart? She loved Hugh, age dif- ference or no, and she felt positive it was a true and lasting love.

But what did any of that matter? He didn't love her back. He had said so.

April sank down on to one of the kitchen chairs and cried, cried till there were no tears left. Then she dried her eyes and stood up, feeling fractionally better. Lifting her chin and taking a deep breath, she turned and resumed her tea-making. April was not one to bash her head up against a brick wall. Nor did she intend to be one of those girls who made fools of themselves by chasing shamelessly after a man. She resolved that once Hugh had had his operation and was back on his feet she would leave it totally up to him if and when they ever saw each other again. Meanwhile, she would go back to university and get on with her life.

Uncle Guy swept in shortly after seven that evening, his flushed face and high spirits showing that the afternoon had not been confined entirely to tea. He was looking well, April thought, though his grey hair and portly figure made him look every one of his fifty-one years.

He raved about April's tan and listened interestedly while she told him a carefully edited version of her holiday and her friendship with Hugh and Harry.

'So, our famous sculptor's being admitted into hospital tomorrow afternoon, is he?' Guy said over a strong cup of coffee.

'That's right.'

'Awful places, hospitals. I remember when I was having my gall bladder operation. The night before I didn't sleep a wink, despite a sleeping-pill. Then the next morning I lay there for what felt like an eternity waiting to be wheeled down into theatre while everyone else was busy eating breakfast and making beds, et cetera. It was sheer hell. I read the whole of *Hunt for Red October* that day. No mean feat, I can tell you.'

'Well, I'm afraid Hugh won't be able to read,' April sighed. Really, she wished her uncle would shut up about Hugh and the operation. She had started feeling nervous about it all again. Over the last two weeks she had pushed aside her initial worries about whether it would be a success or not, trying to take a positive attitude for Hugh's sake. But now that the moment was at hand all her doubts and fears came rushing back. She could imagine how Hugh would be feeling at this very moment, how tense and nervous. It made her want to rush to him, to comfort him. But she had to stay away. She just *had* to!

'I know what!' her uncle exclaimed. 'I've got a couple of talking cassette books in my desk somewhere. You could take them over to Hugh tomorrow morning. You don't have to go back to university till next week, do you? Where did you say he lived? Mosman... Not the best place to get to by public transport. I'll lend you the car again.'

April went to protest, but once her uncle decided something was a good idea there was no stopping him. And if she was strictly honest with herself, deep down, underneath all her common-sense reasonings, she wanted to go.

April swung the Datsun Bluebird carefully into the left-hand lane so that she wouldn't be caught behind the cars turning right at the next big intersection. The lights proved to be green so she sailed through, swinging left slightly on to The Spit Road. She had her street directory open on the passenger seat in case she became lost, but the way to Hugh's house had been etched into her brain after staring at the map for an hour the previous night.

Driving slowly, she easily located Hugh's street on the right and turned into it. Large old trees shaded the footpaths and April noticed that most of the houses, though in faultless condition, were just as old.

Mosman was not a new suburb. It had nestled against the shores of Port Jackson for many decades and the coveted home sites and their solid, family-sized homes had been passed on from generation to generation. During one of their chats up at the cove, Hugh had volunteered the information that his parents' estate had provided him with the family home, along with enough investments for a modest private income.

April's nerves began to get the better of her once she finally spotted number twenty-two. It had a high white-brick wall which totally obscured the house. All she could see as she parked at the kerb was a pitched iron roof and the tops of several leafy trees. A narrow wrought-iron gate stood guard in the centre of the wall.

She had rung the previous evening to say she was coming, and why. Harry had answered, sounding pleased to hear from her. 'Great,' he said. 'You can mind the patient while I pop down to the shops. Hugh needs pyjamas and a new toothbrush for his stay in hospital.'

Levering herself somewhat reluctantly from behind the wheel, April got out and walked over to the gate. There was a buzzer located next to it just above the built-in mail box. She pressed it three times and, as the seconds passed, she became restless and fidgety. It was a cloudy day, but very humid. She pulled her multicoloured top from the waistband of her white jeans, flapping the bottom to let some cool air pass over her sticky skin.

The sudden appearance of Harry's bald head pressed up against the bars nearly gave her a heart attack.

'Hi, there,' he said, slipping the lock and throwing open the gate. He was dressed in a pair of navy surfer shorts and a navy singlet, his fierce-looking face softened by a welcoming grin. 'Hot, isn't it?' he said, dabbing at the perspiration on his forehead with a handkerchief. 'I've been mowing the lawns all morning, and trying to get the place in order.'

April glanced around the large front garden as they walked towards the house together, noting the freshly cut lawn, the neat edges, the perfectly kept garden beds. Harry had shown himself to be a meticulous housekeeper up at the cove and she didn't doubt he'd been working like a dog since his return yesterday. She knew how unkempt a place could get after a few weeks away.

'Everything looks great, Harry,' she complimented, lifting appreciative eyes to run over the stately old home. White-brick and single-storeyed, it had the wide cool front veranda inherent in federation-style homes, with bay windows on either side of a most attractive front door. Such beautiful stained-glass panels were rarely seen these days, not to mention the elegantly carved brass door-knocker.

'Where's Hugh?' April asked casually once they reached the front door.

'Would you believe he's still sleeping?' Harry pushed open the door, revealing a long cool hallway with an exceptionally tall ceiling.

'At eleven o'clock?'

Harry sighed and shook his head. 'He didn't sleep last night, the poor thing. I heard him at three still pacing up and down, so when he finally dropped off I didn't like to wake him. He'll have to get up soon though. Admission at the hospital is between two and three this afternoon.'

'I see,' she murmured, her stomach turning over at the mention of what Hugh was about to face. 'Well, lead me to the kitchen, Harry. I'll wake him with some coffee while you do that shopping you've got to do.'

'You're a life-saver, girlie. A real life-saver!'

Harry moved into the cool of inside, with April following. Despite the home's basic quality, she was surprised to see that the walls needed painting and that the strip of floral carpet running down the hall had seen better days. It was typical of Hugh though, she conceded, that he wouldn't think to spend money on maintenance of his home. He would have other priorities, such as great chunks of marble!

Several shut doors blocked any views of the rooms on either side of the hall and they eventually emerged into an enormous, though old-fashioned kitchen. April was not surprised, however, to see that it was spotless, since Harry was in charge. Hugh, she suspected, would be a typically messy bachelor if he didn't have someone to look after him.'

'Where do you keep the coffee?' she asked, putting her bag on the floor and approaching the myriad cupboards.

Harry opened one of the head-high cupboards that lined the walls. 'And here's the crockery,' he indicated, opening another.

'Thanks. Now off you go. I'll manage.'

'Don't mind Hugh if he's a grouch,' he warned.

'I won't.'

Harry gave her a grateful look, and left.

April smiled ruefully to herself as she filled the rather ancient jug with water. The grouchier, the better, she decided. It was rather hard to feel tender and loving towards a grouch.

Ten minutes later, with a mug of steaming coffee cradled carefully in her hands, April made her way down the hall in search of Hugh's bedroom. Her heart began to thump erratically at the thought of invading such an intimate domain, and as each opened door failed to find Hugh her jumpiness increased.

One room was clearly Hugh's studio, her gaze passing over many more chunks of marble than even she had imagined he might own. Large and small, rough and smooth, all different colours, the room was full of them. Only the large wooden work-table was free of their presence, though it was littered with all manner of things from tools to books to old newspapers to a selection of empty mugs.

April lifted her eyebrows and moved on. The next door on the right proved to be a bedroom, but, it being empty and tidy, she decided it had to be Harry's.

Now there was only one door left. Gingerly she twisted the brass knob, pushing it just far enough to see inside. Hugh was sprawled across a king-sized bed and...

Oh, no, April groaned silently. Once again he was stark naked!

Fortunately, he was lying face down and, while his tanned back and taut buttocks had an undeniable appeal, they were not as disturbing as certain other parts of Hugh's anatomy. April moved closer, her grip on the mug increasing. Keep your cool, girlie, she kept telling herself. It's only flesh and blood.

Yes, she thought drily. *His* flesh and *your* blood, pounding like a hundred drums in your head.

As carefully as shaking fingers would allow, she put the mug down on the bedside table next to his glasses and ever so slowly pulled the sheet out from under his feet and up over his body. She let it drop, as if she were dropping it on a sleeping snake, at waist-level.

She tapped him on the shoulder. 'Hugh . . .'

He stirred, rolling sideways so that the sheet wrapped tightly around him, outlining the contours of his lower body. Oh, God! April looked away sharply, then back, this time at his face only. There was stubble on his chin, shadows around his closed eyes. His thick tawny hair was in disarray. He looked vulnerable yet very, very sexy.

'Hugh!' This time her voice was louder and her hand not so gentle. Was she angry at herself or at him? she wondered.

'What?' He woke with a fright and lurched upright.

'It's all right, Hugh,' she reassured hurriedly. 'It's only me. April.'

'April?' One hand ran unsteady fingers through his hair while the other grabbed rather roughly at the sheet. 'What in hell are you doing here at this hour?'

'It's gone eleven,' she said far too shakily, and firmed her jaw. 'Harry said it was time you were up.'

'Eleven?' Hugh flicked his sightless gaze towards the open door. 'Where *is* Harry, then?'

'He popped down to the shops to buy you some pyjamas. You have to wear such things in hospital, you know. You can't sleep in the raw.'

His head snapped towards her.

'Don't worry,' she said drily. 'You were reasonably decent when I came in.'

His sigh of relief irritated her. What did he think she was going to do? Take unfair advantage of him? Maybe he thought she had deliberately come into his bedroom to feast her lustful eyes on his body.

'Watch it!' she cried when he reached for his dark glasses, almost upsetting the coffee. 'You almost spilt the coffee I brought you,' she said, handing him his glasses, then the mug.

An awkward silence descended while he drank it down. She had the oddest feeling that he was watching her over the rim of the mug, though she knew he couldn't see her at all from where she had moved back to. Agitated, she started looking around the room, admiring the lovely old bedroom suite which looked almost of antique status. 'I like your furniture,' she said for something to say. 'What wood is it?'

'Walnut, I think. It belonged to my grandmother, passed down to Mum, now me.'

'I like your house too. It has character.' And so have you, came the sudden clear thought. What other man would have stopped the other night on the beach, particularly if as frustrated as Hugh had admitted to being? Most other men wouldn't have cared about her virtue or the consequences. Max had called a halt to their possible affair merely because she wasn't experienced enough for him.

'That was good, April,' Hugh said, holding out the empty mug.

She reached for it with both hands, her fingers curling around his. An electric charge pulsated up her arm, but it was Hugh who jerked his hand away, who spun around to sit on the side of the bed, the sheet still firmly in place. She stared at his back, and the way the muscles across his shoulders were stiff with tension.

Heat suffused her skin as she recognised this tension for what it was, and what had caused it. Her touch. Her soft, feminine touch.

But April found no joy in this realisation. Hugh had been perfectly frank about his physical frustrations. He wanted a woman, *any* woman. He had admitted as much up at the cove. The inadvertent brushing of her flesh against his had probably aroused memories of what they had done on the beach together and of what his body was missing. He wouldn't have been human, or the male he was, if such thinking hadn't affected him.

'If you wouldn't mind doing a quick exit,' he said gruffly, 'I'd like to have a shower.'

A *cold* shower, no doubt. But she was only too willing to go, her own body having leapt in response to her thoughts. She too couldn't forget what had happened between them, how he had been able to make her feel before that moment when he had pulled back.

'As long as you can manage,' she said shakily as she made for the door.

'Necessity is the mother of invention,' he growled after her. 'I know where every damned tile, towel and tap is in that blasted bathroom. I spent weeks doing nothing but going from here to there and back again!'

She closed the door on his burst of ill temper and took a deep breath. It was hard not to feel angry, both with herself and him. She could understand his irritation, but that didn't make it any easier to put up with. A moment ago she had wanted to lash out at him, to tell him to go to hell and take his prickly moods with him.

But that would hardly be the action of a friend. And Hugh desperately needed friends, people he could rely on in this time of trial, particularly after his experience with Cynthia. Harry had confided to her that most of Hugh's so-called friends had drifted away during his blindness. Max had lent him his beach-house but Max was, after all, only a business associate. So April was in a no-win situation. If she abandoned Hugh she would feel terribly guilty. But by staying in his orbit she was opening herself up to continuing heartache. And a frustration that would rival anything Hugh was feeling.

April returned to the kitchen, rinsed out the mug, left it to drain on the sink then wandered out on to the back veranda. She stood there for a moment, blinking in the sudden glare of outside before letting her eyes rove around the enormous back garden, a far cry from the ten-by-ten-foot yard behind her uncle's house. One could almost see a cricket match being held on the expanses of lawn.

April sat down on the steps in the shade of wide eaves. What a lovely home this was, a home just right for a whole horde of children. She had always wanted a lot of children, despite her wish for a career as well. Somehow she'd always thought she could juggle both. Now, she didn't think she would have to bother. A deep wretchedness swamped her. It just didn't seem possible that she would ever fall in love again, after Hugh...

A sudden breeze lifted her hair, and April glanced up to see darker clouds gathering on the horizon. The southerly change that had been predicted for later that afternoon seemed to be arriving early. Her attention was drawn to the assortment of clothes flapping on the line. She stood up and walked across, and began unpegging the items, putting them in the trolley under the line.

'April! Where are you, dammit?'

April swung round at the sound of Hugh's voice. He'd come out on the back veranda and was leaning with one hand high on a post, the other clutching a towel around his waist. Freshly shaven and showered, he looked even more breathtakingly handsome. His bronzed torso gleamed where droplets of water still clung, the glistening skin giving extra definition to the well-honed muscles that rippled just beneath the surface.

'I'm here, Hugh. Getting in the washing.'

'I can't seem to find my shorts. Did you pick them up? They were on the floor beside my bed last night.'

'I can imagine,' April grumbled under her breath. 'It looks as if Harry's put them in the wash,' she said more loudly. 'I'll bring them to you. They're quite dry.'

But when she stood on the bottom step and handed up the brightly coloured shorts he seemed to glare down at her. 'I heard that first remark,' he said in a low, curt tone. 'I'll have you know I put the shorts there so I'd know exactly where they were! For pity's sake, April, do you think I like being like this, depending on others to do things for me? I hate it!'

April counted to ten. 'I can understand that,' she said with creditable calm. 'But you won't have to worry about such things after tomorrow, will you?'

'Maybe,' he muttered. 'Maybe...'

His patent doubt softened her heart, but she said firmly, 'You have to be positive, Hugh. The doctors are confident, aren't they?'

'Aren't they always?' he mocked.

She thought of her mother and how the doctors had kept telling her the lump in her breast was most unlikely to be cancerous. But what if it had been? Wouldn't they have been guilty of giving her false hopes?

Still, it wouldn't have done Hugh any good if she told him about that.

'Would you rather they be negative?' she pointed out. 'I wouldn't think so. Besides, I'm quite sure the doctor wouldn't say your operation has an almost one hundred per cent success rate if it hasn't. And Hugh, it's important for you to go into surgery with an optimistic attitude. The mind is a powerful thing. It can make one feel sick even when there's no physical reason to be so. We had a dog once who had its tonsils out. The next day it was fine, simply because it didn't know it should be otherwise. If you go into this operation thinking it isn't going to be a success, then it probably won't be.'

Her lecture finished, Hugh said nothing for a few moments. Then he shook his head. 'You'd better watch it, April,' he drawled. 'If you keep talking sense like that I might forget how young you really are.' And, with that, he turned and stalked back into the house.

April was left staring after him, her mouth suddenly dry. She wasn't sure if she was relieved or not when she heard Harry's voice calling out to them from the front of the house. Hugh's tone and words had conveyed a type of intimate threat that had brought goose-bumps to her skin.

She spun away and strode over to get the washing basket and carried it inside, determined to distract her over-active brain and body with some ironing. But all she could think of was what might happen when and if they were ever alone again, particularly after her got his sight back.

April was not a vain girl but she was honest. And she knew men found her sexually attractive. If Hugh was as frustrated as he claimed to be, would he always be able to resist what she might recklessly offer him once more? She doubted it, doubted it very much.

The thought didn't do much for her peace of mind or her earlier resolution to let Hugh make the running.

'That's some frown you've got there, girlie,' Harry commented as she set up the ironing-board.

She glanced up at him. 'I was just thinking about tomorrow,' she muttered, grateful that Hugh had retreated into his room.

Harry sighed. 'Speaking of tomorrow...'

CHAPTER EIGHT

APRIL had a blinding migraine. She knew the cause. Tension. But it didn't make the blurred vision or the sick pounding in her head any easier to bear. For the umpteenth time she got up from the chair and paced around the hospital room.

'For Pete's sake, April, sit down,' Harry growled.

'I can't.' She continued to walk up and down, up and down. 'I'm worried sick.' April's stomach gave a sudden heave and she dashed into the bathroom that adjoined Hugh's private room. When she returned, she did sit down, white-faced but slightly better.

'Boy, you really meant it, didn't you? About being sick,' Harry said. 'Is there something I can get you?'

She gave him a wan smile. 'No, nothing. I ... I feel better now.'

'I guess I shouldn't have asked you to come and stay with me today. It wasn't fair to you, under the circumstances.'

'U-under the circumstances?'

Harry gave her a look that was remarkably affectionate. 'You don't think I've been blind too, do you, girlie? I know you're in love with Hugh. And I know the fool treats you like some sort of kid.' Harry sat down on the side of Hugh's empty bed, picked up April's hand and patted it. 'Don't worry, he won't think you're such a kid for much longer.'

A flurry of activity in the corridor outside had both April and Harry on their feet. A trolley-type bed was wheeled into the room by a blue-uniformed man, a nurse alongside. Hugh, with eyes bandaged, was lying still and grey-faced under a mountain of blankets.

'Why has he got all those blankets on?' April asked Harry in a worried voice.

The nurse heard, however, and answered while she helped the porter move Hugh into his own bed. 'He woke up in the recovery-room shivering,' she said matter-of-factly. 'Some people react to anaesthetic like that. The body temperature plummets.'

April swayed on her feet and Harry grabbed her. 'Is that dangerous?' he asked as he lowered April back into her chair.

The nurse smiled. 'Not usually. Of course we don't leave them that way, hence the blankets. As you can see, once he felt comfortable, he drifted off to sleep again. Thanks, Warren,' she said as the porter departed with the trolley.

April finally found her voice. 'The operation went well?'

'As far as I know,' the nurse murmured, busying herself taking Hugh's blood-pressure.

'When can we speak to the doctor?' Harry joined in.

'He'll be in theatre for a few hours yet. You might not see him till he comes in later this afternoon to take off the bandages.'

'So soon?' April was astonished.

The nurse began packing up. 'Oh, yes. In this type of operation sight recovery is instantaneous. Once they've replaced the damaged jelly with the synthetic solution, the patient should be able to see.'

'Should' being the crucial word, April thought nervously.

The nurse wrote something on Hugh's chart at the foot of the bed then looked up. 'I have to go now but you can stay as long as you like. If you need a nurse for anything, ring the buzzer.' She lifted Hugh's pillows to show the buzzer lying underneath then moved towards the door, turning briefly before she left. 'Oh, I've left a bowl there on the side-table just in case Mr Davies doesn't feel well when he wakes. If you can't manage, just ring.'

For a few moments all Harry and April could do was stare down at Hugh's unconscious figure. He looked pitifully vulnerable, lying there between the antiseptic sheets, his tanned skin having acquired a pasty, sickly colour.

'Dear God, let him be able to see,' April prayed, and it wasn't till Harry answered her that she realised she had spoken aloud.

'Amen to that,' he finished. 'Can you stay with Hugh for a while, April?'

'Yes, of course.' Wild horses wouldn't have been able to drag her away.

'I thought I might go and get some flowers.' His cheeks went a shade of pink. 'I know that sounds a bit wimpish but I want Hugh to see something bright and beautiful when they take those damned bandages off. Not just white walls and polished floors.'

April found his gesture unbearably touching. This rough, gruff man loved his friend, with a love that urged him to do something he would normally find embarrassing.

'I think that's a wonderful idea,' she said warmly. 'I wish I had thought of it first.' And I wish I shared your faith in the operation, she added privately.

'Hugh won't think it...silly?'

'Oh, no, Harry. He'd really appreciate it, I'm sure.'

Once Harry was gone April moved her chair closer and reached to stroke the damp strands of hair away from Hugh's forehead. He was sweating profusely. Surely he was too hot? She glanced at the numerous blankets and wondered if she should ring for a nurse. Common sense told her it wouldn't hurt if she removed just one. She did so, then turned the other blankets back from his neck.

He stirred. 'Thirsty,' came the raspy whisper.

April saw the jug of iced water on his traymobile and quickly poured a little into the plastic cup. She pressed it to his lips, thinking he would just take a sip, but he gulped down a couple of mouthfuls. It was a mistake. Immediately he retched, and she reached for the bowl in the nick of time. Once he had finished and was lying back, pale and drained, she pressed the buzzer.

A nurse bustled in, saw the problem, and advised no more water for a while. She did, however, take off another blanket. 'After a while he can suck some ice, and, if he doesn't bring that up, then he can have a few sips of the water.' She bustled out with the bowl, returning immediately with a clean one.

'I'm sorry, Hugh,' April said softly.

'April? Is that you? I thought you were a nurse.'

'Hopeless nurse I'd be. I shouldn't have let you drink so much.'

A faint smile flittered at the corners of his parched lips. 'We always seem to be having a problem with drink,' he murmured.

She stiffened at the memories his words evoked, unable to continue. The silence was both awkward and extended.

'You still there?' he asked, a tentative hand reaching along the bed.

She only hesitated the tiniest second. 'Yes, Hugh,' she said, taking his long slender fingers in hers and giving them a reassuring squeeze. I'm still here, she said silently. I'll never leave you. Not unless you tell me to go.

He did not tell her to go, nor did he let her hand go. It rested in his on the mattress, palm against palm, fingers entwined.

'Harry was here when they brought you back to your room,' she said evenly, not at all betraying the way her heart was racing. 'He went out to buy you something.'

'Oh? What else is there for him to buy?'

'It's a personal present, a surprise, and I'm not going to spoil it by telling you.'

'You and Harry are already spoiling me with all this attention. Shouldn't you be at lectures, or something?'

'Nope. I don't go back till next Monday so you'll have to put up with me for the rest of the week. And Uncle Guy said he'd drop in at the weekend, if you're still here.'

'God, I hope not! I've had enough of hospitals to last me a lifetime. But I would like to thank him for those cassettes he sent over. They were a godsend last night.'

'I'll pass on your thanks,' she offered.

'You're a good friend, April. I don't know what I would have done without you and Harry.'

Tears hovered in her big blue eyes. Oh, Hugh... I don't want to just be your friend...

He licked obviously dry lips. 'Could I have a chunk of that ice, do you think?'

She quickly blinked back the tears. 'Just a small piece.' She slipped a bit on to his tongue, but by moving she'd had to drop his hand, and when she sat back down it seemed too forward for her to pick it up again. The feeling of closeness that seemed to be growing between them disappeared with the loss of physical contact, melted away like the ice.

She began to wish Harry would return but by noon he was still absent. A lunch tray came for Hugh, but he said the very thought of food turned his stomach. The meal, a mild curry and rice, looked quite appetising and when April said as much Hugh suggested she have it.

She was indeed hungry, worry having made her skip breakfast, and it didn't take much encouragement for her to give in. Besides, it was something to do and, while eating, she was almost glad to see Hugh drift off to sleep, his head lolling to one side on the pillows. A fortuitous happening, as it turned out, for Harry popped his head in the door shortly afterwards.

'Asleep, eh? Good.' His head disappeared, only to be replaced by the most enormous arrangement of carnations she had even seen. Pink, red and white interspersed with greenery. And that wasn't all. There followed a basket full of delicately hued orchids and then a massive spray of yellow and orange gladioli.

'Couldn't find any blue flowers,' Harry complained. 'The violet in the orchids was the closest I could get.'

'Oh, Harry... Harry... They're lovely.' April gave him an enthusiastic kiss on the cheek.

'Cut that out! Keep the kisses for Hugh.'

April went bright red. 'Harry! Ssh... Hugh might hear you.' Now she was completely flustered.

'So? Do him good to know you love him!'

'No, Harry, no,' she whispered. 'Please don't tell him. Promise me you won't!'

'That you, Harry?'

With Hugh's awakening, April shot Harry a pleading look. He nodded reluctantly before answering his mate. April stifled her sigh of relief. Much as she had fantasised over pursuing Hugh with a more aggressive, liberated attitude, it just wasn't her. That time up at the cove had been an unusual situation, a spontaneous temptation she hadn't been able to resist. But in the cold light of day she knew she had too much pride to throw herself at Hugh's feet. And too much sense. For even if he capitulated, and had an affair with her, it wouldn't last. It couldn't, unless he truly loved her back.

After Harry's return, conversation was kept to what they were going to do when Hugh got out of hospital. Everyone sounded relatively normal but at regular intervals a short, strained silence would descend, betraying their underlying tensions.

Hugh's doctor made an appearance shortly after three. A tall slim man, still in theatre garb, he breezed in with the ward sister and, without further ado, began removing Hugh's bandages. April found herself holding her breath, so taken aback was she by the doctor's speed and efficiency.

'Everything went well, Mr Davies. We'll take these off for a few minutes then replace them for a couple of hours. After that they can stay off, but I would suggest you wear your dark glasses until your eyes stop watering under glare.' He didn't even slow down as the last bandage dropped away. 'There we are. Now open your eyes, Mr Davies.'

Understandably, Hugh didn't spring his eyes open as fast as the doctor ordered. April watched in petrified hope as both eyelids flickered, then blinked, then rose. Can you see? she wanted to scream at him. Say something, Hugh! Oh, please, don't let him still be blind.

His eyes were on her...surely. Staring at her... Was he really focusing, or was it some cruel quirk of fate that made him appear to be looking in her direction? And then his lips moved.

'Blue *and* beautiful,' he whispered.

'What is, Hugh?' she murmured, moving closer.

'Your eyes...'

'Oh...' The tears flooded into those blue eyes with such a rush even she wasn't prepared for them. They spilled over, ran down her cheeks, trickled down the back of her throat, choking off any further speech. She turned her face away with a muffled sob.

'Things have been a bit tense around here,' Harry said in an explanatory way. 'Fact is, I feel a bit like crying myself.'

Oh, kind, kind Harry, April thought as she pulled herself together and turned back, mopping at her eyes.

They were all waiting for Hugh to say something more but he seemed frozen, stunned almost, his gaze jerking away from April to stare almost blankly at Harry's beautiful flowers. Suddenly he blinked, his eyes finally focusing on the various colours of the glorious display. He shot Harry a heart-warming glance.

'Your eyes feel OK?' the doctor asked. 'They appear to be watering a little.'

'They're fine.' Hugh's voice was thick. 'Can't I leave the bandages off?'

'Well, I——'

'Please...' The plea echoed in the room, and even the hardest heart in the world could not have been unmoved.

The ward sister cleared her throat. 'If we turned off these lights and brought in a lamp,' she suggested kindly, 'he should be all right, Doctor.'

'Hmm. It's a mite irregular, but I suppose it'll be all right. Best draw the curtains.'

April hurried to do so and the ward sister went in search of a bedside lamp. She was back within a minute and the doctor was satisfied with the results.

'I'll see you in the morning, Mr Davies,' he rapped out as he walked quickly away, the nurse in harried pursuit.

'He should be a truck driver,' Harry quipped after him. 'He'd never be late with a load, that's for sure.'

Hugh smiled for the first time but he was looking at Harry, April noticed, not herself. 'I gather you're the one responsible for transforming my room into a Garden of Eden?' he teased.

'Who said?' Harry blustered.

'A little bird told me.' Hugh laughed, giving April a lightning glance. Why did she have the awful feeling that he didn't want to look at her? Was he embarrassed now that he was forced to put a face to the voice that had tried to seduce him?

'I thought you might like to see all the colours you've been missing,' Harry muttered. 'The only one I couldn't buy was blue.'

Hugh's eyes turned almost reluctantly back to April. 'That colour seems catered for already, don't you think?'

'You mean girlie's eyes? Yes, I have to admit that it's hard to top them.'

'Oh, go on with you!' she said impatiently. 'It's Hugh's eyes we should be talking about. Isn't it wonderful, Hugh? Aren't you happy?'

Those grey eyes which she'd imagined so long ago to have been blue as well flickered with the strangest expression. She tried to grasp its essence but it eluded her. There was a hint of distress, then frustration, then finally...nothing. She could no longer hope to see it. He had shut out the light, drawn the curtains across his soul.

'Of course I'm happy,' he said in an oddly taut voice.

April glanced at her watch as she came downstairs that evening. Ten past seven. Time to be leaving for the hospital. She hastened her step, popping her head into her uncle's study before she left. 'I'm off now. Thanks again for the loan of the car.'

Guy glanced up from his writing and pushed his reading glasses up on to the top of his head. 'Let me have a look at you.'

April moved into the room with some reluctance. She had gone to a lot of trouble with her appearance, thinking that Hugh might not have been impressed with her baggy jeans and simple T-shirt that afternoon. 'I'll be late,' she said with a nervous laugh.

Her uncle cast a discerning eye over his niece's comely figure, shown to advantage by a lemon cotton jersey dress. It had a rolled collar, cut-in shoulders and a slim, curve-hugging fit. The white leather belt slung around her hips matched her high-heeled white sandals, all of which contrasted with her black hair. A pale bronze lipstick outlined her full lips and a whiff of perfume wafted from her pulse-points.

Uncle Guy sniffed, then frowned. 'You're rather dolled up for a hospital visit, aren't you?'

'Do you think so?' she answered carelessly.

The grey eyes narrowed. 'Yes, I do,' he said curtly. 'What exactly *is* your relationship with our Mr Davies?'

'R-relationship, Uncle? Why, we're just good friends.'

'Just good friends,' he repeated slowly. 'Somehow I don't feel reassured by that comment, my dear. Remember, I *am* responsible for your welfare. I hope you realise that Hugh Davies is a grown man?'

'Yes. As I'm a grown woman,' she countered with far more assertiveness than she usually showed to her uncle.

He looked taken aback for a second, but then he nodded. 'So I see . . .'

'I must go, Uncle, or I'll be late. Bye.'

April felt quite proud of herself as she hurried off. She could appreciate her uncle's concern, since Hugh was far older than the boys she usually dated, but after all she would be twenty-one shortly, and it was *her* life. April *knew* she loved Hugh, knew it wasn't a silly adolescent infatuation as Max had been. Of course, what would happen from this point on she *didn't* know. That was up to Hugh. But nothing was going to stop her from doing her best to impress him as a grown-up young lady, not some flighty girl just out of her teens.

The visiting-bell sounded as April dashed up the steps of the hospital, so she wasn't late. She stopped at the shop in the foyer where visitors could buy gifts for the patients. April waffled over fruit or chocolates and finally compromised. With a box of fruit jellies in her hand, she made her way up the stairs to the first floor, her pulse-rate leaping into overdrive as she approached private room 7b.

April should not have slowed near Hugh's room. If she'd walked right in without hesitating she wouldn't have had to live through such a painful experience. As it was she stopped to catch her breath and steady her nerves, and in that brief span of silence a woman's voice drifted, clear as a bell, through the open doorway.

'Hugh, I can't tell you how much it means to me to see you looking so...fit and well. And to think you can see again. I can hardly believe it.'

'Really, Cynthia?' April's breath caught at the name, and the hard sound in Hugh's voice. 'Forgive me if I say your good wishes are a trifle late.'

'Oh, Hugh... Hugh... Don't be like that. You've no idea what I've been through... The agony... The guilt. It's been hell.'

'It hasn't exactly been a picnic for me either.'

'I know, I know. And you've no idea how sorry I am at the way things turned out. If only I'd been stronger, but when I saw you after the accident, so still, blood all over your face... At first I thought you were dead...' The words shook with emotion. 'I sat with you in the emergency ward at the hospital for hours and hours. I never left you for a minute. You were unconscious most of the time but occasionally you'd half wake in a sort of delirious fog. All you said was..."I can't see, I can't see"...over and over in some kind of ghastly litany. Hugh it—it tore me apart...'

Cynthia's voice broke for a moment, but when she continued it rang out, warm and overwhelmingly sincere. 'I couldn't bear it, Hugh. To see you lying there, broken and bruised. And the intern said you were blind. Nobody told me that there was even the remotest chance you'd get your sight back. I suppose—looking back—that there hadn't been time for them to do the appropriate tests, to bring in the specialists...'

The voice faltered, then resumed, a desperate note trapped in every word. 'Try—please try—to look at it from my point of view. I felt terribly responsible. I... I'd had a couple of vodkas before I came to pick you up that night. I thought you'd hate me for having caused your blindness. Knowing how much your art means to you, I couldn't envisage our relationship lasting. Every time you felt frustrated about not being able to do the things you wanted to do, you'd blame me.'

'Cynthia, I——'

'No, wait! Let me finish. I have to say it all, make you understand. I...I had a nervous breakdown. Daddy sent me to a rest-home overseas. I was there for months. I've only been home a little while. Don't ever doubt that I loved you, Hugh. I did. I loved you. I still do. Even if you never want to see me again...'

April's hand flew to her mouth, stifling the sob that had risen to her lips. She leant back against the wall, her breathing a series of rapid, shallow pants. She wished with all her heart that she had never heard the words Cynthia had just spoken, never heard the undoubtable truth each syllable contained. She said she loved Hugh, and the worst thing was...April believed her. Her action of deserting him had been a disturbed emotional reaction, not the heartless cruelty April had imagined. And if, as April suspected, he was still harbouring feelings for the woman, it wouldn't be long before she was back in his life again.

April could not bear to stay another moment longer. She levered herself away from the wall and hurried along the corridor, the box of jellies clutched to her chest. She fled down the stairs, along another corridor, past the shop, into the foyer. As she hurried towards the open main doorway her progress was halted by a big, rough hand closing firmly over her slender wrist.

'And where do you think you're going?'

Startled, April stared up into Harry's rather angry-looking face.

'Are they for Hugh?' he went on, tapping the box of fruit jellies.

She swallowed and nodded.

'Hmph!' Harry snorted. 'Don't tell me. You took one look at dear old Cynthia and bolted. Am I right or am I wrong?'

April's stricken eyes dropped to the tiles on the foyer floor. 'Sort of,' she husked.

'For pity's sake, don't leave the poor bloke in that bloody woman's clutches!'

April's head snapped up, her eyes flashing. 'What else do you expect me to do? She loves him, and he probably still loves her.'

'Poppycock!'

'Oh, Harry, you're prejudiced!'

Harry clenched his teeth together and looked like thunder. 'Maybe I am,' he muttered, 'but I can recognise a sincere person when I see one. And that Cynthia female is definitely a fraud!'

'Believe what you like, Harry,' April sighed.

'I certainly will! You should have been there when she sashayed into the room a few minutes ago. She looked at me as if I were something that had crawled out from under a stone. Just because I'm dressed like this.' His hand waved over his shorts and singlet. 'She's nothing but a bloody snob,' he went on fiercely. 'Dismissed me as if I were a servant. Said she wanted a private chat with Hugh. And let me tell you something else, April. She'll have a hard job convincing Hugh she really loved him...I saw the fury welling up in those newly opened eyes of his when she walked into that room. Our Hugh's a lot less trusting than he was a year ago, I can assure you.'

'Believe me, Harry,' April said wearily, 'she was coping very well when I left.' She pushed the box of jellies into Harry's hands. 'Here, give these to Hugh, and for God's sake don't tell him they're from me.'

'But he's expecting you.'

'I'm sure you can think of a plausible excuse. Say I was sick or something.'

'Oh, girlie, you're making a big mistake.'

She sighed. 'Harry, I've been making one big mistake after another, ever since I met the man.'

CHAPTER NINE

APRIL was sitting alone at the kitchen table the following morning, forcing some muesli down her throat, when the phone rang. She dashed to answer it before it woke her uncle, who hated being disturbed before nine. 'Hello?' she asked rather breathlessly.

'April?'

Her heart did a complete somersault at the sound of Hugh's voice. Goodness, what was he doing ringing her at this hour? It wasn't even eight o'clock. 'Hugh, what is it? Is there something wrong?'

His light laughter brought instant relief. 'My, but you're a little worrier, aren't you? Nothing's gone wrong. Everything's fine now.'

Fine that he had his eyesight back? Or fine that Cynthia was back in his life? 'Then why are you ringing?' she said far too tautly.

'You mean you don't know?'

'I have no idea.'

'You little fibber! There I was last night, waiting with bated breath for you to arrive, and what happened? All I got was a box of fruit jellies and some pathetic message that you hadn't wanted to intrude when you saw I already had a visitor.'

April was too rattled by Hugh's flirtatious manner to be angry with Harry for not covering for her. 'Your fiancée is hardly any old visitor, Hugh,' she said shakily.

'My *ex*-fiancée,' he reminded her.

'From what I overheard her telling you, that might only be a temporary status.'

'Don't be ridiculous!' he suddenly snapped. 'I wouldn't take Cynthia back in a million years. I don't know who she thought she was, thinking she could walk back into my life after all that had happened and expect me to forgive and forget.'

'But she still loves you!' April gasped, shocked by his angry outburst.

He made a harsh sound that reminded her of one of Harry's grunts. It only confirmed her suspicion that, underneath his anger, Hugh might still be in love with the woman. 'She sounded very sincere,' April said with her stomach churning.

'Look, let's forget about Cynthia, shall we?' he growled, reinforcing April's fear. 'I'd rather talk about you,' he added in a much lighter tone.

'What about me?'

'For one thing, when am I going to see you?' His voice was seductively soft, dangerously sexy. 'I missed you last night, April.'

She swallowed convulsively. This wasn't happening to her. It *couldn't* be real! It was far too close to her dreams, to what she had hoped would happen once he got his eyesight back. Her mind whirled, wanting to believe the emotion vibrating in his voice, but at the same time wary of it. The last thing she wanted was for him to turn to her on some sort of rebound.

'I'm getting out of hospital tomorrow morning,' he went on when she said nothing. 'And I can't wait! I'm dying to get back to work after all those wasted months. But first...'

'First?' she repeated, her heart in her mouth.

'First, I have to buy some new clothes. I have nothing that fits me except a couple of pairs of Bermuda shorts. Harry's come up with some jeans and a sports shirt I can wear out of the hospital, but I can hardly live in those. Would you come with me, April, give me your expert female advice? Harry says his taste in clothes is as pathetic as mine and I need a woman's opinion.'

Now April was confused. Was that all Hugh wanted from her, help with selecting some new clothes? Her heart sank. No doubt she'd misinterpreted his earlier behaviour as flirting. He'd merely been on a high from being given the good news about leaving hospital.

'I'd like to, Hugh,' she said with a sigh, 'but I have to go in to the university tomorrow and buy my textbooks for this semester. If I don't they'll all be gone.'

'Couldn't you go today instead?' he persisted. 'I really want you to come with me.'

'I... I suppose so. But I'll have to miss your afternoon visit. I can't come tonight, either. Uncle Guy needs his car and he won't let me use public transport at night.'

'I fully agree with him. Don't worry about any visiting today. Now that I can see again, it's not so lonely. Harry insisted on renting me a TV.'

'Where do you want me to meet you, then, on the Thursday?' she asked. 'In the city, or at the hospital?'

'How about we meet in the hospital foyer at ten-thirty? I'll get Harry to leave my Rover in the car park.'

They spoke for a few more minutes over nothing consequential but he made her laugh a few times. It rather disturbed her, this new relaxed Hugh. In a way April preferred the short-tempered mocking individual she was used to, for she always knew where she stood with him, firmly in the role of likeable kid and platonic friend, with no chance of anything more. Now she wasn't so sure...

Maybe he *had* been flirting with her earlier. Perhaps Cynthia's turning up had merely confirmed in his mind that he was over her. Maybe Harry had been right, April pondered. Now Hugh had seen she wasn't such a kid, he might want more from her than just friendship.

April was still considering the possibilities when a bleary-eyed Uncle Guy came into the kitchen just after nine. 'Did I hear the phone before?' he asked with a yawn. 'Was it for me?'

'Er—no.' She bit her bottom lip, feeling nervous over her uncle's reaction to her continuing friendship with Hugh. 'It was Hugh, telling me he was getting out of hospital tomorrow and asking me to go clothes-shopping with him.'

Uncle Guy gave her a sharp look. 'And you're going, I suppose.'

She turned steady eyes towards him. 'Of course. Why not?'

He shrugged. 'You're asking for trouble going out with a man as old as that.'

April's chin lifted. 'Hugh's a decent man,' she defended.

'But still a man!' Her uncle snorted. 'And I suppose you're going to ask him to your twenty-first birthday party as well.'

Her coming-of-age was on the following Saturday week, and, while her parents had promised her a big celebration when she went home soon at Easter, Uncle Guy had insisted on giving her a party on the actual day. 'I . . . I'd like to,' she admitted.

His expression showed resignation. 'Very well. I've always held the opinion that when a young person reaches the age of twenty-one it's time they assume full responsibility for their life. Just remember that also means you have to accept all the consequences of your actions.'

April cocked her head to one side and studied Hugh's reflection in the large mirror stuck on the wall. It was safer somehow than looking at the real thing. 'Yes,' she told him. 'That should do.'

What an understatement! Hugh was looking breathtakingly handsome in an outfit she had put together from the casual menswear department at a local department store. A loosely woven coffee-coloured top hugged his chest, the expensive knit fabric not wrinkling at all where it stretched across the broad muscles. Off-white stretch jeans skimmed across his hips then followed the shape of his powerful legs down to the cream canvas loafers on his feet.

The sales assistant who'd been helping them walked over with a jacket in his hands. 'This matches the jeans,' he said, slipping the modern, loosely shaped garment up Hugh's arms and over his broad shoulders.

It looked terrific, as had the other clothes they had decided upon. The pile already included a dark brown casually styled suit, assorted separates, a soft camel-coloured leather jacket, shoes, shirts, socks. But no ties. Hugh refused to wear what he called an outdated utterly useless item.

'Your husband looks well in just about anything, ma'am,' the salesman complimented.

April coloured. 'Oh, but he's——'

'You like this jacket, darling?' Hugh cut in, lifting his sunglasses for a second to wink boldly at her.

April tried not to show how taken aback she was. Since they had met up at ten-thirty in the hospital foyer Hugh had been friendly enough in his manner towards her. But there'd been not a hint of his wanting to develop their friendship into anything more, though wearing those sunglasses did preclude the eye contact a man and woman used to give that sort of message. Now here he was, suddenly expecting her to take part in a joke that implied a familiar intimacy between them.

April was bewildered for only a moment, however, quickly realising that this was just another form of Hugh's old patronising self. It was a type of teasing, putting her on the spot like this. Irritation made her decide to teach him a lesson.

'Oh, I don't know, dear,' she said, tapping a doubtful finger against her chin. 'It's very nice but haven't we spent enough already? The telephone bill came in yesterday and I have to confess it's a mite higher than usual. I suppose I shouldn't have rung Mother in Brazil so often last month. But I thought, how often does one's mother explore the far reaches of the Amazon? I mean, she might not come back, might she?' April directed towards the startled assistant. 'What value can one put upon a mother? I mean . . .'

Hugh strode over and clamped a firm hand over her elbow. 'Now don't get yourself all worked up, darling,' he said through gritted teeth. 'I have enough money for the telephone bill *and* the clothes. We'll take everything!' he informed the open-mouthed man standing beside them.

Hugh was still shaking his head when he pulled his grey Rover up outside his house at Mosman. 'That's the last time I take you shopping, you minx,' he said with a pretend growl, then laughed.

April surrendered to her own fit of the giggles. It had been rather fun, despite her initial pique. 'Did you see the look on that man's face?' she chortled.

'I certainly did. He threw me a pitying glance, I can tell you. Not that he should mind. I was a damned good customer.'

'You did spend a lot, Hugh,' April commented with a slight frown.

'I can afford it,' he tossed off. 'I rang my accountant this morning and it seems my modest inheritance has more than kept pace with inflation this last year. A genius at investment, that man. Besides, I haven't spent much on clothes for years. Come on, let's leave the parcels for the moment and go inside. I think we deserve some coffee. Not only that, I have something I want to show you.'

April laughed. 'Is this another version of "come up and I'll show you my etchings"?'

His face turned slowly towards her and her breath caught in her throat. 'And what if it were?' he asked quietly.

She gulped down, suddenly aware of nothing but the mad thumping of her heart and the knowledge that behind those glasses his eyes were definitely roving over her body. She was wearing the same yellow outfit he hadn't seen the other night and the knitted material now felt hot and clammy against her skin.

'I...I don't think I'd like it,' she said, her voice sounding strangled. But the admission amazed her with its truth. Up till this moment, she had thought she would willingly let Hugh make love to her whenever and wherever he wanted to.

She could see he was frowning now, his forehead wrinkling above the glasses. 'Hugh, I'm sorry if you thought that——'

He stopped her by reaching over and touching her hand. 'It's all right, April. Really. No need for any apology of any kind. I'm glad you're not the sort of girl who leaps into bed with anyone at the drop of a hat.'

'But Hugh,' she said, taking a deep breath, 'I don't think of you as just anyone. You know that. I wouldn't mind if you made love to me...'

He sucked in a startled breath.

'...but only if you really care about me. Not because you're missing Cynthia.'

He took off his sunglasses. His eyes were appalled. 'Is that what you think? That I would use you as some sort of sexual substitute?'

'Not intentionally...'

He gave an exasperated sigh. 'I thought I'd already demonstrated I wasn't that sort of man!'

She shrugged. 'You're only human, Hugh.'

His look was sharp and thoughtful. 'You really aren't so young, are you?'

Her heart leapt but she kept her eyes steady on his. 'I don't think so. But it's what *you* think that matters.'

'Just at this moment,' he muttered, 'I'm not sure what I think...'

'Then perhaps we'd better forget this conversation and go inside,' she went on, her composure the best piece of acting she had ever done. 'Didn't you want to show me one of your pieces of marble?'

Hugh's face showed surprise. 'How did you know what it was I wanted to show you?'

Her smile was wry. 'A person couldn't be around you five minutes without knowing your priorities in life. Your work comes first, second and third, in that order. Anything else would have to be slotted in at random.'

'Is that so?' A single eyebrow lifted, but his gaze dropped to her mouth and breasts before returning to her eyes. 'My priorities have been reassessed lately.'

April was shaken by the depth of desire she saw in Hugh's eyes. 'Come on, let's go,' she suggested nervously, her hand going to the door-handle. 'It's getting hot in here.'

Hugh was laughing as they both climbed out.

April blushed her confusion, unaware that she had made a *double entendre*. 'Did I say something funny?'

'Not at all. Not at all,' he hastily returned, but a drily amused expression lurked in his eyes.

As he led her over to the gate April realised what she had said, and flushed uncomfortably. How odd, she thought, that Hugh's coming on to her sexually should rattle her so! It was what she wanted, wasn't it?

The answer came back straight away. Not quite… She only wanted Hugh as her lover if he really cared about her, if any physical relationship between them was to lead to a more permanent one. Yet that seemed unlikely, for April could not see Hugh having a girl of her age as his girlfriend, let alone marrying her.

Both the gate and front door were locked, prompting April to ask where Harry was.

'He's out looking for a job,' Hugh explained as he ushered April along the cool hallway and into his work-room. 'He said I didn't need a minder any more and he had no intention of being a free-loader.'

April shook her head. 'Isn't that just like him? He pretends to be a hard man but he's not, is he? Perhaps one day he'll learn to trust women again, and fall in love.'

'I doubt it. He was hurt too deeply. Here, have a look at this,' he said, and swept a dustcloth off a piece of marble resting on the work-table. 'Tell me what you think of when you look at it. Tell me what you see.'

April took a deep breath and walked slowly forwards.

It was a roughly rectangular block, bluish grey in colour, with streaks and dots of white running through the top section. It was also completely unworked, a virgin block of stone waiting for the touch of the master.

'Well?' he prompted impatiently.

She ran a hand over the cold smooth surface and immediately it came to her. 'The sea...that's what I see... The surf in storm, with the waves curling upwards, foam along their crests just before they crash on to the shore...' Her voice trailed away and she turned to look at him.

He was staring at her, his mouth open. Then it snapped shut. He came forward and grabbed her, lifting her up and whirling her around the room. 'My God, you're a genius. A bloody genius!'

He plonked her down and dashed over to the table where he bent down to examine the marble from every angle, his hands never still on the object of his passion. April found her heart beating faster as she watched him. Oh, to be that piece of marble, she groaned silently, to have him adore her so thoroughly and so passionately.

'I'll let you name it,' he offered. 'Not now—when it's finished!'

He stalked around the table once more and April had the distinct impression that his creative fingers were already itching. 'I think you'd better take me home now, Hugh,' she said, 'so that you can get back here and go to work.'

His eyes flashed to hers, his expression surprised. 'You understand that I must? You wouldn't be offended?'

She could only smile. 'Would it make any difference if I were?'

'No.' He grinned.

April asked him to her birthday party during the drive back to Balmain, adding that she wanted him to ask Harry as well. Hugh accepted readily but expressed doubt about Harry, who he said hated crowds and strangers. 'I'll do my best to persuade him, though,' he offered.

April had expected him to just drop her off and go, but he asked to come inside and look at the marble basket her uncle had bought. She didn't mind, but she was a little nervous over what cryptic comment her uncle might make about her continuing friendship with Hugh.

No voice called out to her, however, when she let them both in. 'I don't think Uncle Guy's home,' she said with a relieved sigh. 'The basket's on the hall table along there,' she indicated to Hugh. 'Go on ahead. I'm coming. I'll just shut the door.'

He was standing looking at it when she joined him. He gave her a small smile, then deftly slipped the rings into two of the dips in the handle where they swung in perfect symmetry.

'Oh!' she exclaimed. 'Is that where they're supposed to go?'

'Not necessarily... Just another perspective.'

'Hugh Davies, you wicked man!' She laughed, giving him a playful tap on his arm. 'Won't you ever let me forget the stupid things I said and did up at the cove?'

He grabbed her wrist and slowly, ever so slowly drew her to him, his eyes locking on to hers. She stared up into them, instantly breathless. 'I don't want to forget any more,' he murmured. 'I want to remember everything. The way you felt, the way you responded to me. I've wanted to do this,' he rasped, his arms enfolding around her back and pressing her to him, 'since the moment I laid eyes on you yesterday.'

And then he was kissing her, bending her head back and kissing her, taking her gasping parted lips for his pleasure, sending his tongue between them, making her moan as a thousand stars exploded in her head.

'God,' he muttered when he released her mouth.

She looked up at him with a type of bewilderment and anxiety in her eyes. For much as Hugh's kiss had aroused her, it also brought apprehension. 'Hugh, I——'

He placed a finger against her lips. 'It's not what you think, April. My intentions are strictly honourable. I care about you, love, much more than I realised. Am I right in thinking you feel the same way?'

'Oh, Hugh...' She could hardly speak, so great was her joy. 'You—you know I do... I *love* you.'

Again that finger pressed against her lips. 'Let's not talk of love just yet, my sweet. Let's take things slowly. There's no need to rush things, is there?'

April's high took a small down-turn. Clearly Hugh was still worried about her age. 'I'm not as young as you think, Hugh,' she insisted. 'Country girls can be surprisingly mature.'

'So I've noticed.' He smiled wryly, his eyes glancing down at her prominent bust.

She gave him another playful thump. 'Stop that, Hugh Davies! I think that underneath your fuddy-duddy act you're very naughty!'

'Guilty as charged.' He laughed, and went to kiss her again.

The sound of the back door banging startled both of them. They were still looking surprised—and perhaps a little guilty—when seconds later Uncle Guy appeared at the end of the hall. 'Oh, it's you, April. I thought I heard something. I was out in the laundry doing some washing. Hello, Hugh...' Her uncle's rather cold gaze swept over him. 'Nice to see you again,' he said in a voice that held no pleasure. 'Glad to hear the good news about your eyes.'

'Thanks.' Hugh nodded, his swift frown showing he had noted her uncle's coolness. He gave April a thoughtful look. 'I think I should go,' he said. 'What date did you say your party was?'

'Sat-Saturday week,' she stammered, shocked that he meant it to be that long before he saw her again.

'And when does it start?'

'About eight,' she said, her face showing her confusion and dismay.

'Right. Thanks again for your help with the shopping, April. And the piece of marble,' he added. '*Au revoir*, Guy.'

'And you,' her uncle muttered before turning away. Hugh gave a dry little smile, took April's hand and walked slowly with her along to the front door. 'Your uncle doesn't approve,' he said ruefully. 'He probably thinks I'm too old for you.'

'He's just being over-protective!'

'Perhaps.'

'Hugh…' She lifted pleading eyes to him. 'Won't I be seeing you again before my party?'

He gave a frustrated sigh. 'I have months of work to catch up on, April. And your party's only nine days away.' When April went to protest he gave her a soft lingering kiss. 'Trust me,' he said on straightening. 'I want to prove to your uncle that what he's thinking isn't so.'

'And what's that?'

'Exactly what *you* thought. That all I want from you is your luscious young body.'

'But you don't! *Do* you?'

'We-ll…' He grinned. 'I *was* hoping it came with the package.'

Hugh left shortly after, April standing at the kerb, following him hungrily with her eyes till he had driven off and disappeared around the far corner.

She turned away, a groan escaping her lips. Nine days till her party. Nine interminable days. She didn't know how she was going to stand it.

CHAPTER TEN

APRIL returned to university on the Monday but wasn't able to put her mind to the lectures, sometimes a whole hour going by before realising she hadn't taken a single note. She scrambled around afterwards, begging notes from friends, but knowing if she didn't settle down soon her results at the end of the year might not be all she had hoped for.

Hugh delighted her by ringing on the Thursday evening, then astonished her by saying he had finished the surf piece. My God, she thought, he must have been working on it day and night since I last saw him.

'Now I'm on to a much smaller project. The type of thing,' he pointed out, 'that the ordinary person could put in an ordinary room. Some little bird once told me not to go making unwieldy sculpture.'

April laughed.

'By the way,' he went on, 'Harry can't make it to your party. He's taken a job driving coaches to Surfer's Paradise every weekend. He said he was sorry but I think he was relieved. Parties unnerve him.'

'That's all right. I understand. But if *you* don't come, I'll kill you. And don't be too late!'

'Wild horses won't keep me away,' he said, dropping to a low, intimate voice that sent prickles up and down her spine.

April's birthday dawned lovely and fine, her level of excitement increasing with the passing of the hours. She kept looking at the clock, counting off the hours till she would see Hugh again. The only dampener on the day was that she had wanted to buy herself something wonderful to wear but her stringent budget simply wouldn't stretch to party clothes. She would just have to dress up her best black skirt with one of her prettier tops.

By seven she had showered and shampooed her hair and was sitting at her dressing-table in a robe, putting on her make-up, when her uncle knocked on the door. He came in looking sheepish, trying to hide a large, gaily wrapped box behind his back.

'Happy birthday, my dear,' he said, grinning, and whipped the box to the front.

She stood up and took it with some bewilderment. 'I thought I wasn't going to open my presents till later!'

'Aah, but this one won't wait.' He beamed. 'Come on, open it up.'

She took the lid off the box and cried out in delight. 'A dress! Oh, Uncle Guy, you've bought me a party dress!' She drew the obviously expensive creation from the elegantly wrapped box. 'Oh, thank you, thank you!' she burst out and kissed him.

'It should fit,' he said. 'I snuck a dress out of your wardrobe to match your size. Don't let me hold you up, now. I have to go down and get the drinks and glasses ready, and put some music on. But you'd better be downstairs by eight in case we have some early arrivals.'

When her uncle closed the door April stripped off her robe and stepped very carefully into the dress. It was dazzling white, made of a fine cotton with a broderie anglaise border. The style reminded April of the type a tavern wench might have worn in Robin Hood's day, with elbow-length puffy sleeves, a low square neckline and tightly laced bodice. The skirt flounced wide then dipped almost to her ankles.

It soon became obvious that her bra would have to go. April discarded it freely enough and laced the bodice up. But when she glanced at her finished reflection in the dressing-table mirror, she almost died. Good God, she couldn't go downstairs like that, with two mounds of burgeoning flesh spilling out over the top of the neckline. It was almost obscene!

The only solution was to loosen the laces slightly, which settled her breasts into a lower, more comfortable position, though now showing a formidable amount of cleavage. April had never worn such a daring style in her life and, despite the fact that her uncle had bought the dress, when she did finally come downstairs she felt self-conscious in it.

Her uncle was standing behind the small bar in the corner of the front lounge-room, polishing glasses, humming away to a Bette Midler song, when she walked in. His humming came to an abrupt halt. 'Good God,' he gasped, his mouth staying open.

'Don't...don't you like it?' she asked shakily.

'Well, I—er——' He gathered himself quickly, his face falling into a resigned, though rueful, expression. 'You look lovely, April,' he complimented her. 'I'm just surprised how...different...it looks on you from how it did on the coat-hanger in the shop.'

The doorbell suddenly rang out, thereby bringing any further discussion on the dress to a swift halt.

'Someone's a bit early,' Guy muttered. 'It's only five to eight. Answer it for me, would you, April? I haven't finished these glasses yet.'

Her heart began to race as she walked out into the hall. Maybe it was Hugh. She hoped so. Perhaps he was as anxious to see her as she was to see him. She hesitated for a second before her hand went to the knob, taking a deep breath to calm a sudden burst of nerves. But when she saw what this did to her neckline she groaned and stuffed her overflowing bust back down, flattening it savagely with outspread palms. A quavering smile graced her mouth as she opened the door.

Max Goldman stood on the doorstep, a bunch of white carnations in one hand and a gift box in the other.

April's mouth fell open as she looked up at him. He looked as dashing as ever in a trendily printed shirt and cream linen trousers, his blond hair sporting a new semi-spiked hair-cut.

'Hmm,' he murmured, running speculative eyes over her as he stepped under the light in the hall.

He handed her the flowers and kissed her on the cheek. 'Happy birthday, doll.'

April was still standing there gaping when her uncle joined them. 'Max! You made it!' He came up and pumped Max's hand.

'I wouldn't miss April's twenty-first.' Max grinned down at her. 'It means she's officially an adult.' And ready for anything, he managed to convey.

April suppressed a groan. Why on earth hadn't she told Uncle Guy about her encounter with Max? It would have avoided this ghastly situation.

'Amuse Max for me, April. I have to get some ice out of the freezer.'

'I gather you weren't expecting me,' Max drawled when her uncle moved away.

'Hardly.' She made no pretence at being polite. She detested the man.

'I presume Guy doesn't know about us?'

'No.'

He laughed. 'So... You haven't forgiven me yet?'

She stared up at him, thinking what gall he had. But then came the realisation that in his pseudo-sophisticated world there was no such thing as sensitivity. All one could do to protect oneself from the Maxes in this life was to never let them get under your skin. 'Forgive you, Max?' She adopted a bored smile. 'Heavens, I'm grateful to you.'

'Grateful?' He looked amused.

'For saving me from the privilege of being the ninety-ninth scalp on your belt!'

He laughed again. 'You overestimate me, April.'

'I doubt that, Max.' She kept up the light bantering tone, thereby lessening the barbs. 'I will always expect the worst from you and I'm sure you won't ever disappoint me.'

He laughed again. 'Oh, April, you are a delight.' He traced her cleavage with an insolent fingertip, causing her to shrink back in outrage. 'Have you any idea how tempting a morsel you were? And still are... Tell me, then, since it's not me, who *is* the lucky fellow you're wearing this dress for?'

'Does it have to be for anyone?' she countered archly.

His knowing smile told it all.

'You two still standing there?' her uncle said as he bustled past. 'Bring Max in here and I'll get him a drink. April, why don't you open Max's present?'

They moved into the living-room together, Max drawing her down next to him on the enormous semicircular sofa that dominated the room. With a resigned sigh April placed the carnations on the coffee-table and tackled the wrapping-paper of the gift.

'Perfume! How thoughtful...' She smiled up at Max through gritted teeth.

His returning grin showed large white teeth. He reminded April of a vampire, a vampire who preyed on young girls' weaknesses.

'So glad you like it. Mother always said, if in doubt, buy perfume.'

'You have a mother?' April muttered under her breath.

Max wagged a finger at her. 'Naughty, naughty. There I was thinking you'd grown up at last and I find you've just become stroppy. This man of yours must have the patience of Job.'

'Bourbon for you, isn't it, Max?' Guy called from the bar.

'I've moved on to Bacardi, actually,' he drawled. 'With Coke.'

'I thought you'd be a whisky drinker forever,' April quipped, remembering how he had funnelled the Jim Beam down his throat all the time.

'And I thought,' Max whispered, leaning close, 'that you'd be a virgin forever.'

She looked up at him sharply and tried with all her might to stop the heat flooding into her cheeks. Best to say nothing, she thought frantically. Deny nothing. Max was just being Max. 'I'd better take this perfume to my room,' she managed in a splendidly casual voice then sped upstairs, not returning till some more guests had arrived.

By nine o'clock April was convinced Hugh wasn't going to come. She tried not to keep watching and listening for the doorbell by busying herself playing cheerful hostess. She fetched drinks, laughed at jokes and skilfully avoided Max, which was difficult, considering the crush of the crowd. Underneath, she felt sick with despair. If Hugh couldn't make it, he could at least have rung.

The living-room was literally filled to capacity, her uncle having asked a lot of people who had surprised them by all turning up. There were friends of hers from university, neighbours, a few people she played basketball with every winter, some of her uncle's older, more sophisticated set.

Some up-tempo music began to throb, and dancing couples overflowed into the hall, the study, even the kitchen. April was on her way down the hall for more potato chips when she passed Max sitting alone on the stairs, an empty glass in his hands. When he spotted her his free hand shot out, grabbing her wrist and pulling her down on to his lap. 'Come here, o, gorgeous one!' He discarded the glass and slipped his arms around her waist. 'How about coming home with me after the party? We'll celebrate your coming-of-age in style.'

'A few too many Bacardis, Max?' April snapped, and began extricating herself from his octopus arms just as the doorbell sent out its musical announcement.

'Hey, where do you think you're going?' Max growled, his arms tightening.

'That's the door,' she said, trying in vain to free herself.

'So? Someone else will get it.'

'But I——'

'For God's sake, April, will you calm down? You've been acting like a cat on a hot tin roof. Don't be so bloody obvious.'

'Obvious?' she repeated huskily.

'Yeah...obvious. When—and if—your prey arrives, try to be a little more subtle. There's nothing worse than a female falling all over her feet to get to a guy. Very off-putting.'

'And you'd know, I suppose,' she flung at him.

'Sure... Why do you think I was first attracted to you? Despite your sexy little body you had a touch-me-not quality that was quite challenging.'

'Oh, come off it, Max! You and I know only too well why you tried it on me. You'd been left flat and didn't like the prospect of going to bed alone. I just happened to be there.'

'Well, well... You have grown up, haven't you? I wonder how much?'

In true Valentino style he bent her backwards on to the stairs and kissed her.

When she went to beat at his chest, he grabbed her hands in a steely grip, holding them fast, using his free hand to grip the back of her head. He was a strong man with large, strong hands. She twisted her face from side to side but this only seemed to enflame him further, for she could feel his tongue probing even more hotly at her tightly clamped lips.

Her eyes widened as her panic increased. She peered over his shoulder, hoping to find someone to help her, and looked straight up into Hugh's face. In a matter of seconds his expression changed from shock to rage to total disgust.

That he would misunderstand the situation so completely gave April the strength to tear her mouth away. 'Max... *please*,' she choked out. 'Let me go. Hugh's here.'

Max drew back, his hand still gripping hers to his chest. 'Hugh?' He glanced over his shoulder. 'Good God, it's Hugh *Davies*,' he muttered, then raised his eyebrows. 'Well, well...' He released April's hands with an infuriating lack of speed and she hurried to her feet, aware that her face was burning.

She straightened her skirt and tried to stop her chest from heaving too deeply. 'Max was just giving

me a birthday kiss. Weren't you, Max?' she added
with an underlying plea in her voice.

'Naturally—what else? It certainly is a small
world,' Max drawled as he stood up. 'I had no idea
you knew April, Hugh.'

Hugh's gaze raked over Max, then herself. She
felt his regard sweep over her bold cleavage with
definite disapproval. 'The surprise is mutual, Max,'
he countered curtly.

'Oh, April and I are old friends, aren't we, love?
We met up at the cove about a year ago. I suppose
that's where you got to know her as well,' Max
rattled on. 'Well, you look as if your stay up there
has agreed with you, Hugh. Great tan! And your
eyesight's back. Didn't I tell you not to worry about
that? Doctors can perform miracles these days,
can't they, April?'

April made some noise of agreement, her eyes
not having left Hugh for a second. He looked
splendid in dark trousers and an open-necked blue
silk shirt, but it was what he was thinking that was
holding her speechless.

'How long have you been back from overseas,
Max?' he asked in clipped tones.

'Only two days. I was going to ring you next
Monday and find out if you've got your nose back
to grindstone again. After all, it's been almost a
fortnight since your operation,' he finished with a
sardonic grin.

'How well you know me, Max,' Hugh said drily.

'Oh, I don't know...' Max gave April a sly
sideways glance which made her wish the floor
would open up and swallow her. 'I have a feeling

you might have become a dark horse in some regards ... So tell me, did Cynthia get in contact with you?'

April saw Hugh stiffen. She herself was startled by Max's question.

'Cynthia?' Hugh said coldly.

'Yes, I ran into her at the airport in Paris a few weeks back and told her about your impending operation. She seemed shocked and said she would definitely go and see you. Did she?'

'She did,' Hugh admitted tautly.

'I gather her visit hasn't heralded an imminent reconciliation,' Max drawled.

Hugh ignored this comment and turned to April, who was standing there in a growing daze of terror. She had the awful feeling that all her hopes and dreams were disintegrating in front of her and there was nothing she could do about it.

'I would like a private word with you, April,' he announced with far too much composure.

Max chuckled. 'OK, I know when I'm not wanted. I'll go help Guy prop up the bar. And don't forget to give the birthday girl a kiss, Hugh,' he called over his shoulder as he ambled off. 'I think she's been waiting for it.'

They were left virtually alone in the privacy of the narrow staircase, even though the party was thrumming along all around them. Hugh stepped up on to the stair April was glued to, his face instantly thunderous. 'You didn't wait long, though, did you?' he snarled. 'One miserable bloody hour!'

For a few ghastly seconds April could only stare up at him, appalled that he would condemn her so quickly, without even hearing what she had to say.

'I wasn't kissing Max,' she burst out in defence. '*He* was kissing *me*. I didn't want him to. He just grabbed me.'

Hugh's laugh was dry. 'Look me in the face, April, and tell me that's the first time Max has kissed you. After all, when Max says he got to *know* a girl, he means it in only one way. Oh, I know you didn't sleep with him, not literally. But there's plenty of other activities for an imaginative couple.'

April's eyes widened, resentment at his unjust and hasty judgement fuelling a hot anger of her own. 'I've done nothing I'm ashamed of,' she denied hotly. 'I . . . I thought I loved him. I—— '

Any further explanation was cut dead by the look on Hugh's face. But it wasn't fury April saw there. It was total exasperation. And just a hint of despair.

'No more, April,' he said in a tight voice. 'No more. Here . . .' He handed her a small, rectangular gift, wrapped in pretty pink paper. 'Happy birthday.' He went to turn away but she grabbed the sleeve of his shirt. 'You're not leaving?' she asked, frantic.

His cold eyes made her flinch. 'You don't honestly expect me to stay, do you? I'm not a masochist.'

Tears welled up but she refused to let them spill, refused to show this man how much he was hurting her. 'Go, then,' she flung at him, finding some solace in lashing out verbally. 'Get out! I don't want you any more. I don't know why I ever wanted you. You're nothing but a coward!'

He rocked back in astonishment at her attack.

'Yes! A coward! You're afraid to have a real relationship with me. Afraid! Just because I'm young! But you're wrong, Hugh. Terribly wrong. And one day you'll know it. We could have been happy together. I know we could...'

Her voice broke then and tears flooded into her eyes. With a despairing cry she turned and fled upstairs. She slammed the door behind her and threw herself sobbing on to her bed, Hugh's present slipping from her fingers to drop silently on to the carpet.

CHAPTER ELEVEN

THERE were three sharp raps on her bedroom door. 'April? Let me in.'

She lay on her bed, sobbing, unable to answer him. Finally, she heard the door open and close, heard Hugh's footsteps cross the room, felt the mattress dip as he sat down beside her prostrate form. But he made no attempt to take her in his arms, or to deny what she'd accused him of.

'Don't, April. Please don't ... You know I never meant to hurt you.'

'No, I don't,' she sobbed into the pillow. When he said nothing more she turned over and lifted her wet lashes, swallowing to gain more control over her voice. 'I love you,' she cried in a strangled voice.

Pain ripped across his face and he got to his feet, pacing across the room before spinning around and glaring over at her. 'You only think you do,' he said agitatedly. 'In a few months' time it will be someone else. You've already admitted that last year you thought you were in love with Max! For God's sake, April, if I thought there was a real chance for us don't you think I would take it?'

His hands raked through his hair. 'I want you, April. I want you like crazy! But I've seen what happens when an older man becomes involved with a much younger woman. I've seen the jealous scenes, the childish tantrums, the sexual manipulations. I don't want that. I want peace and security. And a sense of serenity. I need that for my work. I certainly don't want to have to worry if I'm going to wake up one day and find out that the woman I've given my heart to has grown tired of me, and wants out. Neither do I want one of those casual relationships based on nothing more than sexual gratification. I'm thirty-four years old. I want marriage. Marriage and a family. And a wife mature enough to stick it, even when things get tough.'

April sat up abruptly, her feet curling up underneath the billowing skirt of her dress. 'As Cynthia stuck it out when things got tough?' she pointed out mercilessly. 'Your mature old Cynthia?'

Hugh's jaw clenched hard and he looked away. 'There were mitigating circumstances in her case,' he ground out.

April was shocked that he would find excuses for the woman when he wasn't giving her an inch. 'My God, you're still in love with her, aren't you?'

His eyes jerked back to her, hard and angry. 'If you believe that then you're even younger than I thought! I'll have you know that Cynthia showed up on my doorstep tonight, just as I was leaving for your party. She begged me to let her talk, to explain further. I heard her out and I did feel slightly sorry for her, but that was all. Don't you see? I came here...to you...'

April couldn't see anything any more, except that it was all hopeless and futile. 'I don't know what for,' she said, her voice devoid of all emotion.

'Neither do I,' he pointed out coldly. 'I ought to have my head examined. But I kept telling myself that you were different. God! What a fool I am! At least I now understand why poor Garrick did what he did.'

A wretched despair snaked around April's heart. He hadn't believed a word she'd said about Max. He didn't want to believe her.

She gazed up at him, anguish in her eyes. Oh, Hugh...you really are still blind.

'Don't look so desolate, April,' he said harshly. 'A girl like you won't be lonely for long.'

She dropped her eyes again, not wanting him to see the misery in them. When she looked up again she had carefully replaced the misery with a type of offhand indifference. 'How right you are, Hugh.' She uncurled her legs and got to her feet, brushing the pretty skirt down into place. 'I've already had one proposition this evening. I might take Max up on it.'

His anger was so sudden and swift that April was caught unawares. 'You are not to have anything more to do with Max Goldman, do you hear me?'

Her chin flew up, her cheeks flushed. 'And who are you to tell me what to do? You're not my father or lover. You're not even my friend any more!'

He was glowering at her, his hands bunched into aggressive fists at his side. 'April—don't be stupid— Max has a shocking reputation... I couldn't stand it if he——'

'If he what?' she cut in savagely, pain and resentment making her lash out. 'Took what you so nobly rejected?'

'For God's sake, April, you couldn't! Not a man like that!'

'Why not?' she argued blindly. 'I would think he'd be a good lover. He's had enough experience. A girl needs her first man to know exactly what he's doing, to...'

Her voice trailed away as she saw the control go out of Hugh's eyes. A manic determination had taken its place. He advanced towards her, each step full of frightening menace and passion. 'You can't give your virginity to a man like that,' he rasped. 'I won't allow it...'

She backed away from him till her legs touched the side of her bed. Her hands fluttered up to protect herself. 'Hugh...I didn't mean it—I wouldn't...'

But it was too late.

He grabbed her wrists and pushed her back on to the bed, covering her body with his body, her mouth with his mouth. His powerful legs pried her thighs apart and she could feel his arousal pressing against her even through her clothes. April was truly shocked. Shocked, and almost frightened. His lips were forcing hers open quite brutally, his tongue thrusting deep inside with a passion bordering on violence. She could hardly breathe as this onslaught on her mouth went on and on, punishing, bruising, suffocating...

With a desperate burst of resistance she dragged her mouth to one side. 'Hugh, no!' she gasped.

His head jerked back up immediately, and she was sure he was going to stop. But as he held himself above her, his body stiff and poised, she saw that his eyes were wide and glazed. Naked desire smouldered in their depths, a desire that was beyond reason, beyond conscience.

The knowledge that she could do this to him brought its own brand of insidious excitement. Her heartbeat quickened. Heat sizzled along her veins. From deep inside emerged the inevitable acceptance that she no longer wanted him to stop.

At first his gaze was riveted to her panting lips, but then it dropped down to where a single breast had half escaped its loosely laced prison. She also looked down, witnessing with a dry-mouthed fascination that the exposed tip was growing hard and erect even as they both watched.

She knew he was going to touch it; waited for his hand to move, a tremulous anticipation quivering throughout her body. But when his head began to descend and she realised what he was about to do, she found herself literally holding her breath. And when the tip of his tongue encircled the sensitive point, a shudder rippled through her, the long-held breath erupting from her lungs in a ragged groan.

Once again his eyes snapped up to hers, raking them with a blind anxiety. Surely he didn't think she wanted him to stop? came the dazed thought. If he did, she would die.

Her lips parted. 'Do it again,' she pleaded huskily.

He moaned, his mouth swooping to do as she asked, over and over again, sending a thousand shivery delights through her body. She felt her breast swell, the engorged nipple pouting ripely for

his repeated ministrations. When he sucked the
entire areola deeply into his mouth, a sharp pang
of pleasure dragged at her womb, squeezing her
muscles tightly inside. And in that moment she
gained a tantalising glimpse of how it would feel
to have him take her, fill her. She would welcome
his hardness, enclose him round with the fierce
possessiveness of love.

All of a sudden she wanted both her breasts free,
wanted his hands on her naked flesh. She ripped
at the bodice, the laces. Hugh caught her urgency,
helping her push the now gaping material back over
her shoulders.

'So beautiful,' he murmured, his hands reaching
to knead both breasts softly, then more roughly.

April was in a delirium of desire. She didn't know
what she wanted next, but when Hugh lifted her
skirt and drew away her lace briefs her focus was
soon on that moist pulsating part of her that she
knew would not be still till it joined with Hugh.

When he touched her there she let out a ragged
sigh, her body quivering as the most exquisite sensations rippled through her. She was soon liquid
fire, burning with love for him, her arousal telling
him more clearly than words of the intensity of her
desire. But when he bent his mouth to her heated
flesh, his kiss sent her mad, making her twist and
turn in an agony of longing that was beyond
bearing.

'No, no,' she gasped, and thrust him aside.

She tugged impatiently at his clothes, kneeling
up to help him strip from the waist down. Her hand
came out, quite unconsciously, to touch him, to

marvel at his manhood. It seemed so natural to bend forward and kiss him, as he had kissed her, to show her love, to give him pleasure.

And it did give him pleasure. He closed his eyes, unable to suppress a deep, shuddering moan. When she did it again he grew still and tense, only the sound of his ragged breathing punctuating the electric silence.

The knocking on the door splintered the quietness like the crash of thunder.

'April? Hugh?' Guy's voice was crystal-clear through the door. And very impatient. 'Are you in there? April, your guests are waiting for you to cut the cake!'

April saw Hugh's eyes fly open, witnessed the horror of his appalled self-recrimination. 'Oh, God,' he groaned, and spun away from her. He reached hurriedly for his clothes. 'Fix your dress,' he threw over his shoulder.

'We'll be down in a moment, Guy,' he called, his words clipped.

'Don't be long,' her uncle shot back.

In the ensuing silence they heard his angrily retreating steps.

April felt embarrassed, shattered, confused. 'Hugh, I——'

'Don't say a word,' he snapped, whirling to face her as she was fumbling with the laces on her bodice. 'Not a bloody word!' He was already stuffing his shirt in his waistband.

She held the gaping sides of her dress together with trembling hands. 'But, Hugh, we love each other——'

'No!' He strode over to the door and spun round. 'No,' he repeated. But the anger had drained from his face, replaced by a bleak wretchedness. He turned the knob and yanked the door open. 'Goodbye, April.'

And, without a further backward glance, he left.

April would never know how she got through that night. Obviously there was a part of every person's psyche, some hidden survival mechanism that took over when one's pain became too much to bear, but when one had to go on.

She came downstairs, dry-eyed and smiling. She blew out candles, cut her cake, laughed at all the usual birthday jokes, even helped her uncle clean up afterwards, making some pathetic excuse about Hugh's departure.

Later, she sat alone on her bed, still dry-eyed. She didn't seem to be able to feel. But then her foot brushed something on the floor and she idly bent and picked it up. It was Hugh's present. Just as idly she ripped the paper off and exposed the exquisite little sculpture.

It was made of streaky black marble and looked like a figure eight lying on its side. There was a tiny card tied to it with a pink ribbon which had a word written on it. INFINITY.

April stared at the brilliance of the piece, the way it had been carved so that the grain in the marble followed the curves, never crossing, never ending, the material matching the concept.

Infinity... forever... never ending... Like her love for Hugh. Her crazy, hopeless love for Hugh.

The tears came then, gut-wrenching and loud. April turned and buried her face into her pillow.

CHAPTER TWELVE

IT WAS late on a Saturday afternoon in May, nearly three months after the party, when the phone rang and a paler, thinner April went to answer. 'Yes?' she asked lifelessly.

'April?' There was doubt in Max's voice. 'Is that you?'

'Yes. It's me.'

'You sound down, love. Anything wrong?'

April made a concerted effort to perk up and sound normal. 'No. Not at all. Why?' She had no intention of unburdening her soul to the likes of Max.

'No reason. You just sounded odd, that's all. Is Guy there?'

'Sorry. He's away for the weekend with some wine-tasting buddies of his. They've gone up to the Hunter Valley.'

'Damn. I was hoping he could pop in to my gallery later this evening. A few up-and-coming artists are showing selected pieces—tasty morsels of what the public can expect in years to come.'

'It's a bit late to be sending out invitations, isn't it?' April said archly.

'Yes, but I didn't know till an hour ago that Hugh would want to show something and I thought your uncle might give a critique of it in that column of his. He really liked Hugh's work the last time. But don't worry, it probably won't matter in the long run. The way Hugh's going at the moment there might not be much more stuff of his to write about anyway.'

'Oh? Why's that?' April tried to sound mildly enquiring, but her heart had turned over at the mention of Hugh's name, and she was immediately worried by the concern in Max's voice.

'I gather things didn't work out between you and our temperamental artist, did they?' Max drawled.

'No,' she said tightly. 'They didn't. And what do you mean, temperamental? I would have thought now that Hugh could see again he'd be too busy for temperament.'

Max sighed irritably. 'Yes, I would have thought so too. But it appears that's not the case. That bruiser who lives with him tells me Hugh's been having trouble putting his mind on the job. Not sleeping well and generally being as miserable as sin.'

Just like me, April thought, and a weird feeling coursed through her body. If Hugh was so upset, wasn't it possible it was because of her, because he hadn't forgotten her any more than she had forgotten him?

'Then what is the piece Hugh wants to show?' she asked with her heart in her mouth.

'I have to tell you, April, it's simply the most fantastic thing he's ever done. It looks like the waves in a huge sea just before they crash on to the shore, all menacing power and movement. You can't stop looking at it as though any second the waves will come to life, curl right over and go thump!'

'What . . . what's it called?'

Max made an impatient sound. 'Nothing!'

'Nothing?' There was a tightness growing in her chest.

'Yes! An "unnamed work", he's labelled it. I tell you, April, he's turned into one hell of a difficult man. His looks might have improved but his manner certainly hasn't. He practically bit my head off when I tried putting some pressure on him to give a title to the thing.'

'And Hugh will be at the gallery tonight?' she asked huskily.

'Well, yes, but——'

'Would you mind if I dropped by instead of Uncle Guy? I could give him the low-down on everything.'

'Yes, of course, but——'

'What time?'

'Oh, any time after eight.'

'I'll see you later, then,' April said, and hung up.

Max frowned down into the dead receiver, wishing April hadn't rushed off like that. He'd wanted to tell her Hugh wasn't coming on his own tonight. He was bringing Cynthia with him. But then he shrugged. If April wanted to make a fool of herself then who was he to try to stop her?

April took a taxi to the gallery. Not because she could really afford it but because she had promised her uncle never to take public transport at night, particularly on a Saturday night.

Max's gallery was right in the city, down near the Rocks. It was as pretentious and tasteless as

Max, with revolving glass doors and marble columns at regular intervals, and not a hint of Australian style or culture about it. Yet it was called the Australiana Gallery. But Max knew all the right people and did very well for both himself and the artists who were lucky enough to exhibit in his mausoleum.

April had done the best with her appearance she could, choosing to wear a straight black skirt and a long-sleeved scarlet blouse that looked like silk but was really polyester. The colour suited her and put some life into her face, which was looking more than a mite peaked these days. Not even full make-up could totally disguise the drawn pallor of her skin, or the dark shadows under her eyes. But despite all this the taxi driver ogled her every step of the way as she walked up the steps to the glass doors.

The gallery was crowded, a haze of smoke greeting April as she stepped from the revolving doors. Her gaze travelled over the chatting, drinking, laughing, puffing groups, her stomach in knots. At that moment, she earnestly wished she hadn't come. Whatever made her think she would achieve anything? Even if Hugh had once loved her, it was *her* love he didn't believe in, not his.

It didn't take April long to see Max. His tall blond head was bobbing from group to group, an outlandish black and white striped shirt making it impossible to miss him. He spotted her standing there and started forward, his arms opening wide, a broad smile on his face. 'April! Darling!'

He addressed her so loudly that all the people nearby stopped and stared.

It was then that April saw Hugh near one of the marble columns. And the blonde clinging to his arm.

She had never seen Cynthia before. But she knew immediately who the blonde was. The hairs on the back of April's neck stood up as her eyes moved over the woman with the classic though cold face. She was wearing a slender black dress that had money written all over it, her blonde hair swept back and up, revealing an elegant gold necklace and matching earrings.

April watched Hugh say something and extricate his arm to walk towards her, looking incredibly male in his camel-coloured leather jacket and dark brown trousers, a cream silk shirt underneath. As he drew close though, April saw that the bones in his face looked stretched across his cheekbones. He looked tired. And angry.

'Hello, April,' he said tautly. 'What brings you here tonight? Is she here with you, Max?'

'Not at all,' Max admitted. 'Look, excuse me, will you? Someone is waving to me.'

'You don't have to stay with me, Hugh,' April said stiffly. 'Go back to Cynthia, by all means.'

Hugh's frown was immediate. 'I didn't realise you and Cynthia had met?' he asked, confirming his companion's identity.

'We haven't. I—er—saw her from a distance that night at the hospital.'

'I see . . . Speaking of hospitals, April, you don't look well. Have you been sick?'

Yes, she longed to tell him. Sick at heart. For you, my darling. 'I...I did have the flu recently.'

'You need to eat up. You're too thin.' Thin or not, his eyes kept scrutinising her closely, and he appeared to have to drag them away.

April's heart began to pound when she saw Cynthia approaching. 'Darling,' the woman said, 'don't you think you should introduce me?' That hand went back to Hugh's forearm like a homing pigeon.

'Of course. Cynthia...meet April Jamieson. April...Cynthia Underhill. April was very kind to me during my blindness,' he added stiffly.

The woman didn't seem in the least bit embarrassed at being indirectly reminded how lacking *she* had been at the same time. Immediately, any belief April had once had in the woman's sincerity went out of the window.

'How very kind of you,' Cynthia was saying with a honey voice and eyes like ice. 'Hugh, there's a photographer here wanting to snap you beside your new work. Have you seen Hugh's latest sculpture, April?' she went on in a slightly condescending tone. 'Or aren't you interested in art? Most young people aren't.'

The woman's emphasis on the word 'young' brought April's hackles up. 'I wouldn't be here, Cynthia,' she answered sweetly, 'if I weren't. In fact I'm deputising for my uncle who writes the "Around Town" column.'

April got the distinct impression that this news soothed Cynthia somewhat, for she actually smiled—with her eyes this time. 'Oh, I see. Come on, Hugh. The photographer's waiting.'

April watched Hugh endure the photo session with barely held patience, after which he just stood and stared at his unnamed work while Cynthia drifted to one side to chat to Max. April stared too, a lump forming in her throat as she took in the way Hugh had made her suggestion into a living, breathing work of art.

She moved to stand beside him without even being conscious of doing so. 'It's truly magnificent,' she whispered.

He glanced across at her and their eyes met.

'Why *are* you here, April?' he asked abruptly.

She was going to repeat her excuse, but then she thought, Why bother? This was definitely her swansong where Hugh was concerned and it deserved the truth. Her smile was the epitome of grim resignation as her eyes ran over him, taking in his face and form as though imprinting them on her brain forever. She wasn't to know that she looked at him with a desperate desire that tore into his soul and shattered his bleakly held defences. 'I had to try one last time, Hugh. I had to find out if you still...' she went to say 'loved', then she realised Hugh had never said he loved her '...wanted me,' she finished.

'And if I do?' he bit out, his whole body stiffening in one last frantic attempt to deny what was sweeping through it.

'You know where to find me,' she husked.

'So I do, April.' He looked away from her, unable to bear looking at her for another second. 'But there again, I have all along...'

All her hope died. He might still desire her, but not enough. Not enough... She couldn't go on, an inner quaking beginning to take hold of her. She spun away, head held high, her partially blurred gaze searching and finding Max. She lurched towards him, ignoring a startled Cynthia, drawing Max aside with a trembling hand. 'Get me out of here, Max,' she choked out. 'Please...'

His strong grip fastened around her elbow and in seconds he had propelled her, not outside as she had meant, but into his private office. With the door safely shut he pushed her into an armchair. 'I'll get you a drink,' he said.

April could only nod and bury her face in her hands. She accepted the whisky with shaking hands, gulping it back on to an empty stomach. It burned like hell but in seconds she felt marginally better, certainly more in control.

But she jumped nervously to her feet when Hugh suddenly burst into the room. Max merely raised his eyebrows. 'Can I do something for you, old man?' he drawled.

'I'd like to speak to April. *Alone*!'

'Sure.' Max shrugged. But he took his time pouring himself a whisky and downing it before leaving.

April watched with a dry mouth as the door shut and Hugh started to pace up and down the room. He ground to a halt in front of her, his face in obvious torment. 'All right,' he growled. 'You win. Let's go...'

'Go?' she gasped.

'Don't play games with me, April. You knew when I saw you go off with Max that I wouldn't be able to stand it. It was your final gambit, wasn't it? Make the sucker so jealous he'd no longer be able to think straight. But what the hell? It worked. So come on...' He grabbed one of her hands and began dragging her towards the door...

She wrenched her hand away, stopping with face aghast. 'No!'

His face hardened, if that was possible. 'No? You dare to say *no* at this point?'

April was all hot fluster. 'Well, I... I...'

'You want me to make love to you, don't you? That is why you came here tonight, isn't it? That is what this is all about?'

April gaped at him.

'Don't tell me you're angling for *marriage*?'

April was totally speechless. This wasn't her Hugh talking. This was some sort of madman!

'I didn't think so,' he scorned. 'Marriage is for stuffy old fuddy-duddies. But don't worry, I've changed my mind on that score. I've decided to join the modern generation and give in to what I want, when I want it, without strings, without commitment. And I want you, April Jamieson, naked and willing in my bed. I want to make love to you for hours on end, I want to take your virgin body and make it respond to me in every possible way I can think of.' He grabbed her then, wrenching her hard against his heaving chest. 'Is that what you wanted to hear?' he rasped. 'Is that what you wanted me to say? I'll say anything you want me to say as long as I can have you...'

He groaned then, his mouth claiming hers, covering and possessing it with the passion and hunger of a starving soul, drinking in the soft sweet moisture of her lips and mouth with ragged, sucking gasps. He kissed her over and over, ravaging her lips till they felt swollen and bruised.

Initially April was rocked by the violence of Hugh's passion, and the anger behind it, but she gradually realised it was directed more at himself than her. He'd been fighting her love since the beginning, fighting this deep-seated mistrust of it. But the protective shell he had put around himself had been well and truly pierced now, and April had no intention of letting Hugh retreat behind it ever again. She would bind him to her sexually, make him need her body and the pleasure he found in it. And slowly, eventually, he would learn to trust, and the sort of love she really wanted from him would flower and grow openly in his heart.

She began stroking the back of his neck, kissing him back, letting her body speak for her. I love you, it said. Love you...

Hugh pulled away from her mouth with a moan, his hands trembling as he pressed her head against his chest and raggedly stroked her hair. 'Do you have any idea what you do to me?' he rasped. '*Any* idea?'

'Yes,' she whispered, looking up at him with eyes wide with arousal, lips parted with expectation.

'God...' Hugh let out a quivering sigh before tasting those willing lips once more. 'I want you, April,' he murmured against her mouth. 'Now...tonight. Come away with me. We'll go somewhere private. I'll ask Max for the keys to his beach-house. We can be there in a few hours. There'll be no traffic.'

A shiver of wild exultation ran through her as she thought of being totally Hugh's at last. 'Yes...oh, yes,' she cried.

'Wait here,' Hugh commanded. 'I'll go and speak to Max. Now don't move!'

CHAPTER THIRTEEN

THEY were over the Harbour Bridge and on the expressway heading north when April finally remembered Cynthia. She looked over at Hugh, who'd said nothing since he'd bundled her into the Rover and taken off. 'Hugh?' she said nervously.

'Mmm?'

'What about Cynthia?'

'What about her?' His glance was sharp. 'I asked Max to take her home.'

'And she didn't *mind*?'

'Why should she?' he almost snapped.

'Well, I ... I ...'

'There's nothing going on between Cynthia and me, if that's what you're thinking,' he elaborated with a degree of exasperation. 'I only brought her along tonight because Max insisted I bring someone and she's the only woman I could think of. She was well aware it didn't mean anything.'

'But she called you darling!' April reminded him. And dripped all over you, she didn't add.

'Cynthia calls everyone darling. April, I told you that I would never get involved again with Cynthia,' he went on impatiently, 'and I meant it! I never did entirely swallow her story. Oh, I think she felt guilty enough but as for her so-called nervous breakdown ... I have it on good authority that she spent quite most of her time overseas at ski resorts and on the Riviera.'

April sat in shocked silence.

'Cynthia, I've come to realise since, is a cultural groupie. She likes mixing with people of an artistic bent. Marriage to an up-and-coming sculptor was right up her alley.' He slanted April a sardonic glance. 'Women like Cynthia don't really love. They make suitable choices. Not that I can talk. I can see now that I never really loved her either. She fitted my idea of the perfect wife. Attractive, intelligent, independent, socially competent. Supposedly mature. Perhaps I deserved what I got.'

'I don't think so, Hugh. No one deserves to have done to them what Cynthia did to you. That was cruel.'

His eyes flicked her way. They grew amazingly warm and loving as they scrutinised her, and April's remaining doubts dissolved on the spot.

'I know you wouldn't have left me like that,' he said thickly.

'Never,' she whispered.

A tiny black cloud passed across his face. 'Tell me, April, have you been seeing Max at all?'

Her heart sank till she realised that what Hugh was asking was fair enough. Hadn't she worried that he'd resumed his relationship with Cynthia?

'I haven't seen Max since my party, Hugh. To tell the truth, I haven't been out anywhere except to university since that night. I haven't wanted to.'

Hugh's expression conveyed both relief and surprise. And a new respect. 'I haven't been at my best either. You know, April, I haven't been able to work. I haven't been able to do much of anything.'

'I...I noticed you didn't name that surf piece,' she said somewhat gingerly.

His sigh was oddly soothing. 'Ah, but I'd promised that to you.'

'But...'

He gave her a look that melted her insides. 'Deep down, I must have known I would come for you, April. Eventually...'

'Oh...'

'Now shut up, darling, and let me drive. I'm beginning to get a mite impatient...'

'It's cold,' she said as she climbed stiffly out of the car five hours later. They had made the trip in remarkably quick time but to April it had seemed to last an eternity.

Hugh looked thoughtful as he joined her. 'Max's place will be like an ice-box.'

April shivered. 'I know where Uncle Guy keeps a hidden key. His place is much smaller and he has two quick-heating radiators. He wouldn't mind.'

They walked quickly across the loose sand, arm in arm, their breaths showing mist under the sharp moonlight. A fresh breeze ruffled April's hair.

'I'll make us some hot chocolate,' she offered, once they were inside and the heaters were on. But as she went to walk away Hugh caught her wrist, bringing her back to enfold her into his chest. April's hands slid around and up his back and, when she looked up at him, her heart was hammering against her ribs in breathless anticipation.

The trip up, the having to wait, all the time knowing what was at the end, had brought her to a height of sexual awareness that the longest foreplay could hardly match.

'No hot chocolate,' he said with surprising calm. 'No more waiting...'

'I... I'm a little nervous,' she admitted.

'No need,' he murmured, one hand coming up to brush her hair back, to hold it there on either side of her face while he bent to kiss it. First on the forehead, then her eyelids, then her nose, each cheek, her chin, before sliding down her throat.

'Hugh,' she groaned, her lips parting impatiently.

He gave a low sexy laugh but didn't kiss her. 'No,' he refused, three fingertips pressed against her tingling lips. 'I've spent five hours regaining sufficient control over my body. I don't want to waste it. And I will if I kiss that rapacious mouth of yours.'

'Rapacious?' she repeated with a frown.

'Yes... Rapacious. Greedy. Insatiable.'

'But I want you to kiss me,' she moaned.

'I will—at the right time. First I want to undress you, to see all of you, touch you. With my eyes open this time...'

His hands went to her red blouse, easing it out from the confines of her waistband before starting at the bottom button and working slowly upwards. April tried to stay as calm as he seemed to be but she didn't feel calm. She could hear her heartbeat in the silence of the room, feel a trembling running up and down her thighs. 'Shouldn't we go into the bedroom?' she asked breathlessly.

'If you like,' he said and led her into the smaller room, which was already comfortably warm with the large strip-heater on the wall on full.

He turned her to a standstill at the foot of the low-slung water-bed, her calf muscles resting against the wooden frame. The last button gave way to his questing fingers and he drew the two sides of the blouse apart, his eyes narrowing with concentration on her as he pushed the garment back off her shoulders and peeled it down her arms. There was a slight hitch when it reached the cuffs, which were still done up, but with a brisk tug the sleeves finally lurched over her wrists and Hugh tossed it aside. It fluttered to the floor in a corner.

'That happens to be my best blouse,' she reproached huskily.

'I'll buy you a hundred blouses,' he said, his voice now almost as thick as her own.

Light fingers feathered up her arms and over her shoulders, then across the bones at the base of her neck, then finally downwards to trace the swell of her breasts. Hugh made no attempt to remove the confining skin-toned bra, seemingly fascinated by the way her full curves were lifted and pressed together by the light silky harness. 'You have beautiful breasts, April,' he murmured, moulding his hands around the cups like a human bra.

She swallowed against the tumultuous feelings that were clamouring to be set free inside her, feeling impatient with Hugh's slow lovemaking. But eventually she recognised and surrendered to the strangely addictive pleasure contained in such a gradual build-up of tension. In the end she wanted to wait as long as he was making her wait. She could well imagine these incredible sensations growing and growing till she would be nothing but a trembling incoherent creature who would allow any caress, any intimacy, anything at all. For this was the way she loved him. Totally, madly, mentally and emotionally, physically and sexually. She wanted what he wanted, and if he wanted to take forever making love to her then she wouldn't object.

But that was before his thumbs started rubbing over her nipples, before those normally small, soft buds suddenly burst into hard, swollen instruments of the most exquisite torture. 'Oh, God,' she moaned, and swayed beneath his touch.

He steadied her with a firm grip on her upper arms, watching her with such hot, smouldering eyes that she closed hers, blocking out the evidence of his desire. Hers was bad enough to cope with. His would only make it worse. She almost sighed with relief when she felt his hands on the back of her bra, felt the clasp give way and the garment drawn from her.

From her dark, sightless world she was surprised at the awareness she had of her unfettered breasts. They felt extra heavy and deliciously sensitive, their aroused state craving the return of Hugh's attention. But of course it wasn't his hands she wanted on them. She yearned for those throbbing points to be sucked into his hot moist mouth where they would be nipped and tantalised till she would practically scream for him to stop. She could almost feel the wet lips now, keeping each nipple imprisoned in turn while that wet flickering tongue encircled and licked with a relentless intensity.

Her moans came as a surprise, and her eyes flew open, shocked to find that her fantasy must have stopped being a fantasy some time back. Her hands went to his bent head, her fingers twining through his hair, holding him there, pressing her knees back against the bed to keep from sinking to the floor.

Finally that tormenting mouth abandoned her breasts and travelled downwards, Hugh sinking to his knees and kissing her stomach while he freed her of her skirt, then her shoes, her tights, and finally her bikini briefs. There was no shyness in her as she watched him throw them aside. She wanted to be naked before him, wanted his hands on her most secret places, wanted whatever he wanted.

She felt his hands parting her thighs, felt the knowing intimate touch of his lips and tongue. And then she was moaning and shaking, so much so that he stopped what he was doing, bringing a whimper of disappointment to her lips.

But once Hugh stood up and smiled down at her she was glad he had stopped, glad he had saved that ultimate pleasure for when his body was joined to hers. He scooped her up into his arms and lowered her gently to the swaying surface of the water-bed. 'Just relax,' he told her, and began stripping off his clothes.

But telling her to relax was like telling her not to breathe. Her love, her need, had made her only half of the whole. She was not going to be content till they were as one, till she had been satiated with the ecstatic sensations she knew she would find in his body.

Her hunger grew as he revealed himself to her eyes so that by the time he joined her on the wildly undulating bed she clasped him to her with frantic hands. His need seemed to be equal to hers now, for he didn't return to any aggravatingly slow exploration of her flesh. He positioned himself between her thighs, his elbows on either side of her chest, his hands cradling her face. 'I thought I could last longer,' he rasped, a rueful smile coming to his lips. 'I can't.'

'Good,' she sighed.

He laughed. 'You are a wicked little devil, do you know that?'

'Yes,' she agreed impatiently, arching her body up to rub herself against him. 'Yes, yes, yes!'

His raw naked groan was music to her ears. 'I don't want to hurt you,' he rasped.

'You won't,' she assured him.

April welcomed him. She closed her eyes tightly shut, waiting for the pain. But no cry was torn from her lips this time, only a gasp of surprise at the relative ease with which he entered her.

'Open your eyes, April,' he said thickly, and when she did he captured her parted lips in that long-awaited kiss. Her eyes widened as he began to move in her, his tongue and body thrusting as parallel forces, filling her, driving her mad. With swift savage surges she was transported into another world where straining bodies reached blindly and instinctively for those magical and sometimes elusive moments which had kept man and woman coming together since time began.

They struck with incredible intensity, April's body being gripped by the most sharp, piercing sensations. Her flesh convulsed and contracted around Hugh's, impelling him immediately into an explosive climax. He gasped away from her mouth, shudder after shudder running through him from his toes upwards, ending with an animal cry being punched from his throat.

And then he groaned—a deep, contented groan. And April knew he was feeling as she was feeling, as if she were sinking, sinking, her muscles all heavy languor, her mind a lazy haze of utter bliss. He sagged down on top of her and she held him close, stroking his passion-damp skin with tender hands, telling him how much she loved him.

April woke to find herself alone. There was a note on Hugh's pillow. 'Gone for a walk,' it simply stated.

She lay back on her pillow and sighed, but it was not the sigh of a woman in any distress, or with any regrets, more the sigh of a woman who had been made love to very, very well. April's heart contracted as she thought of how many times they had already made love, and of the various erotic ways Hugh had pleasured her.

The clock on the bedside chest said it was two in the afternoon. She had been asleep only a few short hours but she felt marvellous, simply marvellous.

April stretched and climbed out of bed, aware of her body in a way she had never been before. Her breasts felt heavy and extra sensitive, her skin flushed and tingly. There was a slightly swollen feeling between her thighs. She made her way slowly into the shower, knowing full well that Hugh would only have to touch her and in an instant she would be ready for him again.

The water played over her head and she shut her eyes. Her hand groped for the shampoo, finding it at last on the shelf. But before she could pour any on to her hair the bottle was taken from her hand.

'Let me do that.'

Her eyes flew open to see a naked Hugh standing there, smiling at her.

She laughed. 'Did you go for a walk like that?'

He glanced down at his body which was quickly becoming aroused. 'Well...not exactly like that.'

April laughed again. And Hugh stepped into the shower. She watched, suddenly dry-mouthed, as he trickled a small stream of the soapy liquid over her breasts. Gently, as though moulding a precious piece of clay, he began massaging, stroking the undersides, encircling one aureole at a time, then, finally, grazing lightly over the waiting, aching tips.

April moaned.

He bent into the shower stream that was running over her face and licked the water from her lips. 'You'll never guess what's happened,' he said between brief, tantalising kisses. 'I think my mental block is over. While I was walking just now, creative flashes just kept popping into my head. I could hardly believe it.'

She smiled up at him with adoring eyes. 'I'm so happy for you,' she whispered.

'Not as happy as I am. But I know who's responsible,' he said huskily. 'You are, April. You are... I love you, my darling. I love you...'

'Oh, Hugh...' April's joy knew no bounds.

His hand stroked her cheek. 'Without you I can't function, can't think. I want you in my life, dear heart. I *need* you. Not just for a weekend. But every day, every night...'

'I want to marry you too,' she choked out.

His groan was tortured. 'No, April. No... That's not what I meant.'

'Not...not what you meant?' she repeated, feeling sick.

'I won't marry you at this stage,' he explained haltingly. 'You—you're so young, my darling. So very young... You don't realise how much people can change in their twenties. Their ideas, their needs... It would be very selfish of me to tie you down at this point in time. Move in with me, live with me. And then, in a year or two...'

April stared up at him, finding it hard to hide her dismay. It wasn't her he was trying to protect. It was himself. He still didn't trust her love. Still...

She thought about the decision she had made last night and for a split second doubt and regret reared their ugly heads. But then she dismissed them. She loved Hugh. She knew she did. Eventually, he would know just how much.

*   *   *

'Oh, Hugh, it's simply wonderful!'

April was admiring his latest piece, a semi-abstract version of a horse and rider, called 'Rodeo', with the horse up on its hooves, back arched, trying to throw its rider. Hugh had been working on it all week, with April having barely sighted him.

April placed it down on the kitchen table then stepped back, looking at it from a distance.

'One of the best you've ever done!' she enthused. 'It even looks good in the middle of that old table.'

Hugh came up behind her and began nuzzling into her neck, whispering seductively what he would prefer to do on the kitchen table at that moment.

April's senses leapt in heady anticipation. It had been like that ever since they had returned from their weekend at the cove and started living together. Hugh would come out of one of his creative binges and immediately have this intense hunger for her. He was already turning her around and unbuttoning her shirt.

'It's just as well Harry moved in with Uncle Guy,' she murmured. Then gasped. Hugh's lips had found a nipple.

Guy had been furious with Hugh when he'd brought April home on the Sunday night and announced they were going to live together. But Hugh had asked to speak to Guy alone and, when they had come out of the study ten minutes later, it seemed they had reached some sort of truce. Though still not thrilled, Guy had given April his blessing.

April's parents, however, had not yet been informed, her hesitancy betraying a lingering fear that Hugh might not truly love her after all. Oh, yes, they were sexually attuned, there was no doubt about that. And their enjoyment in each other's company had increased with each passing day. But whenever she brought up the matters of marriage, or commitment, he deftly changed the subject, usually by making love to her.

So when April rang her family every week, she talked of everything else except Hugh, saying to herself that she would tell them about him, *after* she had graduated at the end of the year, and *if* she and Hugh were still together.

A black cloud passed over April's soul and she shuddered. Hugh stood up straight, holding her by the shoulders and staring down at her. 'Is something wrong? You seem ... tense.'

She thought of her visit to the doctor the previous day. 'No,' she said truthfully. 'There's nothing wrong.' The doctor had said she was the picture of health and that pregnancy suited her.

Of course April had suspected she was pregnant for some time, while Hugh had no idea. It had been easy to hide the possibility from him because he lived such an odd life, with odd hours. When he worked, he worked feverishly, only coming out of his studio for food. Days went by sometimes without their making love, which meant she hadn't had to explain her missing periods.

April looked at Hugh's dark frown and wondered what he would say when she told him. She knew he had assumed she was still on the Pill and it worried her terribly that the news would cause trouble between them. Her original idea that a baby would show the permanency of her love now seemed naïve.

The insidious thought came that she didn't have to tell him about her pregnancy yet. She was only two months. Pushing aside a rush of qualms, she reached up to kiss him lingeringly on the lips. 'Now, where were we?' she invited.

His relief was instant, his returning kiss unexpectedly fierce. She found herself edged back till her buttocks were hard against the table. Hugh's hands had returned to her breasts, caressing them none too gently. They were extra sensitive with her pregnancy, and it took all of her control to let him continue. The pleasure was mixed with unexpected pain.

When he suddenly stopped she almost cried out with relief. But he also stopped kissing her and was looking down at her breasts. 'You've put on weight,' he said.

April shut her eyes, her stomach twisting. She should have known he would notice. He was a sculptor after all, with a sculptor's hands, a sculptor's sense of shape and proportion.

'But I like them this way,' he murmured thickly. 'Lovely and full and heavy. You were too thin before.' He cupped one and kissed it with his eager lips. 'Luscious.'

Relief flooded her when she realised he hadn't jumped to any conclusion, but in no time she couldn't stand his energetic attentions any longer.

It was beyond pleasure now. 'Don't,' she cried, and wrenched away.

He jolted back from her as though she had struck him. 'Don't?' His face hardened, his eyes narrowing with suspicion.

April groaned with the realisation of how quick he was to misconstrue her rejecting him physically as heralding a deeper rejection.

'Oh, Hugh,' she sighed. A mental picture of his eternal mistrust of her love flashed into her mind, depressing her unbearably. She had been fooling herself all along. Their relationship wasn't going to work. It *couldn't* work. How could it without mutual trust?

'It's not that I don't want to,' she said, but her hands were slowly rebuttoning her blouse. 'But my breasts are terribly sore. You see, Hugh...' She lifted a resigned face to his. 'I'm pregnant.'

He just stared at her, his eyes oddly unreadable. Shock was all she could determine. 'Pregnant? But...*how*?'

Her smile was weary. It seemed cruel to say, 'The usual way.' Instead she explained quietly, 'I went off the Pill after my birthday party, Hugh. I didn't see the point in continuing with it at the time.' She had decided to see if her periods were still painful, since that had seemed the only reason left for staying on the drug, and had discovered that they were now much lighter, as sometimes happened.

He kept staring at her, but his shock had turned to thoughtfulness. 'So you knew...from the beginning...that you would probably get pregnant.'

'Yes.'

His frown darkened. 'Why didn't you tell me you'd gone off the Pill?'

She shrugged. 'You wanted me, Hugh. That night. As desperately as I wanted you. I had to make a snap decision. I did.'

'But April, there are other forms of contraception!'

Her sigh was an admission. 'I know...but I wanted everything to be...perfect. I didn't want——' She broke off, giving the matter some more honest thought before continuing. 'The truth is, Hugh, that underneath it all I wanted your baby. I love you, Hugh, and I know you love me, in your way, but I guess I didn't believe you would stay with me. I was afraid that one day you would find some reason for us to break up. I wanted to have a permanent part of you to love and keep. I know you will call that stupid and romantic and im-mature of me, but I don't look at it that way. I do love you. And I'm only sorry that you don't believe that my love will last.'

April was astonished at her composure. She had delivered her heart-breaking speech without a tear and as she watched Hugh, standing there dumbfounded, a special kind of satisfaction washed through her. She had sounded as mature and grown-up as she felt.

'Well, Hugh?' she prodded.

He looked down at her with a deeply thoughtful expression on his face. 'I have only one thing to say to that, April. Only one thing....'

'What?' she asked, her heart pounding.

A slow smile creased his mouth. 'Will you marry me?'

CHAPTER FOURTEEN

'DID you know today's our first anniversary?' April said to Hugh.

He gave her a puzzled glance.

'Since the day we first met,' she explained. 'Up at the cove.'

His laugh was light and happy. 'I thought you meant since our marriage.'

'It'll be our sixth-month wedding anniversary shortly,' she reminded him.

And what a wedding it had been! Nyngan had talked about it for weeks afterwards, Hugh having paid for the biggest reception the small town had ever seen. It turned out he was a good deal more well off than even he realised, that investor of his having brought off a recent coup on the commodities market.

'Hey—ssh!' Hugh darted a glance towards the busy hospital corridor then down at the precious bundle in his arms. 'You don't want people to hear we had a shotgun wedding, do you?'

April was still laughing when Uncle Guy and Harry stamped into the room. The two men were like the odd couple, she thought as she looked at them. One so dapper, the other a real navvy. But they had become good friends since Harry had moved into April's old room, the arrangement suiting them well with Harry taking over April's housekeeping chores in exchange for free board. He still drove buses every weekend and was in the process of building himself a small studio for his own sculpting out of the old laundry shed in Guy's backyard. April's uncle was also teaching him how to read and write.

'A little something for the bonnie babe,' Guy announced, placing several packages on the bed.

April glanced ruefully at the large teddy-bear Hugh had come in with, not to mention the other toys her family had brought when they'd flown down the previous day. She shook her head. 'Rachel is going to be spoilt rotten,' she announced. 'And she's only three days old!'

Uncle Guy raised his eyebrows. 'Nothing's too good for my great-niece,' he defended.

'And nothing's too good for my god-daughter,' Harry joined in, coming over to have a closer peep at the sleeping infant.

'Want a hold?' Hugh offered.

Harry looked appalled. 'Hell, no, I might drop her.'

'No, you wouldn't, mate,' Hugh encouraged him. 'Here—put one hand behind her neck, then another behind here...'

Harry succeeded at last, but looked so nervous and shaky even April was relieved when he handed the baby back.

'I think we'd better open these presents, don't you?' she suggested. 'Yours first, Uncle Guy.' She tackled the paper on a large box with gusto. 'I wonder what this is...' She lifted the lid and stared, then looked up exasperatedly. 'Now what do you think Rachel is going to do with a soccer ball, Uncle Guy?'

He was taken aback. 'I thought it was a netball!'

All the other presents were almost as silly, from the electronic robot to Harry's toy train set. 'Didn't anyone tell you that I had a *girl*!' April glared in mock disgust.

'Did you hear that, Hugh?' Guy huffed. 'You've married a sexist. Actually you're a brave man, Hugh, marrying her at all. Do you know what she said to me when I didn't approve of her moving in with you? She said she was going to, no matter what I said. She said she was grown woman, it was her life, her choice, and if I didn't like it then I'd have to lump it!'

'Oh, Uncle Guy,' April protested. 'I wasn't as bad as that!'

'Maybe not.' He grinned. 'Just as well Hugh reassured me that he was only giving you some time so that you could be sure. He said he would have married you that very night if it was only his happiness at stake.'

April turned wide eyes to her husband, who raised his eyebrows and smiled at her. See? his expression said. You were wrong about me.

She sighed and shook her head in wonder and happiness.

It was an enjoyable hour, but by the time Harry and her uncle left April was tired. Rachel, also, was getting fractious, having woken hungry.

'She needs a feed,' Hugh observed, when Rachel kept sucking her fingers ravenously.

'Yes, but . . .'

Hugh smiled his understanding. He picked the baby up from the crib and handed her over to her mother. 'Here... Give the child what she wants.'

Not always, April decided privately. She had no intention of spoiling her children. But she conceded that this hardly applied to food. She pushed back her nightie, unhooked her maternity bra and offered her breast to the hungry infant.

April closed her eyes and breathed in sharply when Rachel started to suckle with even more vigour than usual.

'Painful?' Hugh asked softly.

Her eyes flew open. He was watching the whole procedure with undisguised fascination. 'Not so much now,' she admitted. 'It was bad yesterday. It seems the sucking helps the womb contract back into shape.'

Hugh shook his head. 'Incredible thing, nature.'

He resumed watching Rachel in studied silence.

April's loving gaze rested on her handsome husband, recalling the incredibly forceful way he had directed their lives once he had accepted the reality of her love for him.

They had been married within a month, but there was no honeymoon—April was to apply herself to her studies. Her career was just as important as his, he had said. During the next few weeks he had had the house renovated, with one of the bedrooms being converted into a nursery. He had taken over most of the housekeeping chores and learnt to cook, since April vetoed any help in the house. But the most astonishing decision he had made was not to do any sculpting in the months leading up to the birth, saying he would devote all his time to her needs for once.

And he had been as good as his word, April conceded, though she had detected a certain impatience during the last few days before she went into labour. She suspected he was itching to get his little chisel back to work.

April looked down lovingly at her baby, thinking to herself that she didn't regret giving up the job at the *Herald* to look after Rachel. She had the satisfaction of passing her final exams with distinctions and was very happy staying at home with Hugh and the baby for the time being. Perhaps later on she would...

Suddenly Hugh jumped up. 'I have to go.'

'Go where?'

'Home... I have this perfectly brilliant idea. You know that big chunk of light brown marble I've got? I'm going to do a large piece—sorry about that, I know you like small ones—I'll call it "Mother and Child", or something original like that... I see the woman with her head tipped back, her eyes closed, a look of controlled pain on her face. And the child at her breast, greedy, demanding... I must get at it...' He was already halfway out of the door.

'What about a goodbye kiss?' she protested.

His glance was full of passion. 'You'll have to wait for that,' he growled, then grinned. 'By the time I finish this, it'll be worth waiting for.'

April was left staring after an empty door. For a moment she was annoyed, and then she relented. He'd spoilt her, of course, these last few months.

Hugh was what he was and, after all, she and their child had been his inspiration.

She looked down at Rachel who had drifted off into blissful sleep. 'It's just as well we're going home tomorrow, bubs,' she said in wry warning. 'I have a feeling that if we weren't, we wouldn't see your father for quite some time.'

She rubbed her cheek lovingly over the silky down of her baby's head. 'But the end result is worth waiting for,' she murmured. 'All the best things in life are worth waiting for...' A sweet smile of satisfaction curved her mouth. 'Though sometimes you've got to give things a little push along. It's a matter of conviction...and love. Love is certainly worth pushing for.'

April sighed in contentment and closed her own eyes.

BARBARY WHARF

An exciting six-book series, one title per month beginning in October, by bestselling author

Charlotte Lamb

Set in the glamorous and fast-paced world of international journalism, BARBARY WHARF will take you from the *Sentinel*'s hectic newsroom to the most thrilling cities in the world. You'll meet media tycoon Nick Caspian and his adversary Gina Tyrrell, whose dramatic story of passion and heartache develops throughout the six-book series.

In book one, BESIEGED (#1498), you'll also meet Hazel and Piet. Hazel's always had a good word to say about everyone. Well, almost. She just can't stand Piet Van Leyden, Nick's chief architect and one of the most arrogant know-it-alls she's ever met! As far as Hazel's concerned, Piet's a twentieth-century warrior, and she's the one being besieged!

Don't miss the sparks in the first BARBARY WHARF book, BESIEGED (#1498), available in October from Harlequin Presents.

WELCOME TO

The quintessential small town, where everyone knows everybody else!

Finally, books that capture the pleasure of tuning in to your favorite TV show!

GREAT READING...GREAT SAVINGS...AND A FABULOUS FREE GIFT!

Each book set in Tyler is a self-contained love story; together, the twelve novels stitch the fabric of the community. The covers honor the old American tradition of quilting; each cover depicts a patch of the large Tyler quilt.

With Tyler you can receive a fabulous gift, ABSOLUTELY FREE, by collecting proofs-of-purchase found in each Tyler book. And use our special Tyler coupons to save on your next TYLER book purchase.

Join your friends at Tyler for the seventh book, ARROWPOINT by Suzanne Ellison, available in September.

Rumors fly about the death at the old lodge! What happens when Renata Meyer finds an ancient Indian sitting cross-legged on her lawn?

If you missed *Whirlwind* (March), *Bright Hopes* (April), *Wisconsin Wedding* (May), *Monkey Wrench* (June), *Blazing Star* (July) or *Sunshine* (August) and would like to order them, send your name, address, zip or postal code, along with a check or money order for $3.99 for each book ordered (please do not send cash), plus 75¢ postage and handling ($1.00 in Canada), payable to Harlequin Reader Service, to:

In the U.S.

3010 Walden Avenue
P.O. Box 1325
Buffalo, NY 14269-1325

In Canada

P.O. Box 609
Fort Erie, Ontario
L2A 5X3

Please specify book title(s) with your order.
Canadian residents add applicable federal and provincial taxes.

TYLER-7

JAYNE ANN KRENTZ

A two-part epic tale from one of today's most popular romance novelists!

Dreams
Parts One & Two

The warrior died at her feet, his blood running out of the cave entrance and mingling with the waterfall. With his last breath he cursed the woman— told her that her spirit would remain chained in the cave forever until a child was created and born there....

So goes the ancient legend of the Chained Lady and the curse that bound her throughout the ages—until destiny brought Diana Prentice and Colby Savager together under the influence of forces beyond their understanding. Suddenly they were both haunted by dreams that linked past and present, while their waking hours were filled with danger. Only when Colby, Diana's modern-day warrior, learned to love, could those dark forces be vanquished. Only then could Diana set the Chained Lady free....